'I said, what about your family, Rowan? Can you tell me anything about them?'

Nervously Rowan brushed a hand across her face to break the contact of the searching gaze that seemed to burn her skin where it rested. 'I—— No, I can't. I've tried all day and. . .' Her head swam as she looked into those deep, dark eyes. 'I can't remember, Nathan!' It seemed as if her life beyond this house, this man, had never existed. 'I know you think I'm lying——'

'No, Rowan. You let slip something you hadn't told me before and I had to be sure that there wasn't anything else. I want to help you, but you have to let me. You have to help yourself.'

Tell him! her conscience screamed at her.

'Let me ring your family, Rowan. Let me at least contact them and tell them you're safe.'

'Not yet,' she whispered weakly.

'What are you running away from?' Nathan's voice had sharpened noticeably. 'What are you so afraid of?'

Books you will enjoy
by KATE WALKER

LEAP IN THE DARK

Kidnapped by a stranger along with the two children she was looking after, Ginny didn't know where to turn for comfort. The worst thing was, all her instincts were telling her to turn to Ross Hamilton—and he was the very man who held them captive. . .

JESTER'S GIRL

From the minute he set foot in the restaurant she owned, Daniel Tyson had antagonised Jessica Terry. But though she reacted to him as a stranger, there were two things she didn't know. One was the unusual way he made his living—and the other was that they'd met—and fought—once before. . .

RUNAWAY

BY

KATE WALKER

MILLS & BOON LIMITED
ETON HOUSE   18–24 PARADISE ROAD
RICHMOND   SURREY   TW9 1SR

First published in Great Britain 1990
by Mills & Boon Limited

© Kate Walker 1990

Australian copyright 1990
Philippine copyright 1990
This edition 1990

ISBN 0 263 76579 2

Set in 10 on 10½ pt Linotron Times
05-9002-57628
Typeset in Great Britain by Centracet, Cambridge
Made and printed in Great Britain

CHAPTER ONE

THE house came into sight just as Rowan was about to despair. Footsore, dejected, and feeling thoroughly exhausted, she had been close to sitting down at the side of the road, burying her face in her hands and weeping like a baby, and it had taken all her strength to force herself to walk just a few more yards.

Just round the next bend, she'd told herself, then you can sit down. And it was as she rounded that bend that she saw it; red-bricked, large and imposing, and seeming like some impossible, glorious gift from Fate.

At first, with her head buzzing with fatigue and the faintness that came from hunger, Rowan could not quite believe that it was real. She had been walking for hours without a sign of human habitation, without even a single car passing her on the exposed moorland road so that she could thumb a lift. Not that she looked like the sort of person anyone would want to pick up, she had to admit. Her short black hair was a bird's nest of tangles and mud as a result of the fall, which had also left a nasty scrape down the right side of her face, and the skirt of her formerly crisp white dress was ripped and covered in green grass stains. The cotton shirtwaister, while cool and smart for work, was totally unsuited to a long hike along country roads, and its appearance hadn't been improved by a night spent sleeping fitfully in the car.

Rowan shivered as a chill wind crept under the scarlet lightweight jacket that she wore over the dress. Yesterday, the blazer had been more than adequate in the warmth of an early spring sun, but now the weather had taken a turn for the worse and the dark clouds gathering overhead looked distinctly ominous. If only she had had time to go home, grab something warmer.

But then, yesterday, she hadn't been thinking clearly. In fact, she hadn't been thinking at all beyond the need to get away—*far* away—and escape from Colin's threats. She hadn't even paused to check that she had enough money in her purse, or, failing that, at least to make sure that she had her cheque-book and card which, too late, she had remembered were lying on her dressing-table at home.

Home. Weak, despairing tears stung Rowan's eyes and her slender body slumped despairingly. Would the house where she had lived with her mother and stepfather ever be home to her again? When Bernard found out what she had done—because surely by now Colin must have told him—would he ever want her in his house again? She had betrayed his trust, destroyed his confidence in her, so wasn't it most likely that he would want nothing at all to do with her?

Rowan's small, heart-shaped face grew white and pinched with distress, the clear blue eyes that normally gleamed like sapphires under her thick dark lashes became cloudy and dull as her full, soft mouth compressed tightly against the cry of desolation that almost escaped her. Only now did she realise what she'd done; that by running away she'd played right into Colin's hands. When he knew she'd gone there would be no reason at all for him to hold back what he knew. Thwarted in his ugly scheme, he would inevitably want his revenge and would take a great delight in recounting all the sordid details to her stepfather.

If only she'd had the courage to go to Bernard first and admit the truth. But she hadn't dared. Instead, she'd panicked, thinking only of getting away from Colin and rushing out to her car, not caring where she went, simply wanting to put as much distance between them as possible. She didn't even know where she was. The last time she had seen a signpost had been just before the car had run out of petrol on this deserted road, and she had been walking for miles since then.

But now the house stood ahead of her, as welcome

a sight as an oasis to a traveller in the desert. Rowan licked her dry lips, wishing she hadn't thought of that particular image. She hadn't had anything to eat since breakfast yesterday, and the few pounds she had had in her purse had only been enough to buy two gallons of petrol and a single cup of coffee at the motorway services that she had stopped at before taking an exit at random to end up here.

Surely whoever owned that house would give her a glass of water, at least, and then——

And then what? She could ask to use the phone, ring a garage and get them to come out to her car— except that she wasn't at all sure just where her car was, and she hadn't the money to pay for any petrol. One thing was certain, she couldn't phone home to ask for help—she had cut off that retreat once and for all.

But she couldn't stand here any longer. Already the first heavy drops of rain were beginning to fall. She would be drenched to the skin if she didn't get under cover soon. With an effort that made every aching muscle cry out in protest, Rowan forced her legs into a stumbling run.

It had seemed so much closer from the road. She hadn't bargained on the winding drive that sloped upwards towards the main door, adding extra, exhausting yards to her journey. The infrequent drops of rain had turned into a heavy downpour, and within seconds her thin clothes were soaked through, her black hair hanging in dripping tendrils round her face, her smartly fashionable sandals squelching inelegantly by the time she stumbled up the steps and pressed her finger to the bell.

With a sob of relief she heard its ring echo throughout the house. In her urgency she had pressed far harder than she had ever intended, and the noise seemed loud enough to wake the dead. Was there anybody there? Oh, please, *please*, let someone come soon!

The silence from inside the house stretched Rowan's

nerves to breaking-point. Had she finally found a refuge, only to discover that there was no one at home? A wild flurry of slashing rain drove her into frantic action as she pressed her finger to the bell once more and left it there.

'Please! Please answer! Oh, please let there be someone there!'

The sound of the bell was so loud that she didn't hear the footsteps crossing the hall, didn't hear the handle turn, so that the first indication of the fact that she had been heard came when the door swung open with an unexpected suddenness that had her falling forwards, blundering headlong into a hard, powerfully built form.

'What the hell——?'

Husky masculine tones, rough with shock, penetrated the whirling haze that filled her mind as firm hands came out to hold her upright, hard fingers digging into her arms through the thin, soaking material of her jacket.

'Who are you? What do you want?'

'I. . .'

The rush of relief at not being alone any more was almost more than Rowan could cope with. Her mind seemed to be slipping out of focus, spinning sickeningly, her eyes blurring so that she had to blink hard in order to be able to see him at all.

She had a brief, uncertain glimpse of a tall, rangy frame, dressed in a dark grey pin-stripe suit of such superb cut and quality that it could only have been tailored exactly to his measurements, an immaculate white shirt, unbuttoned at the throat, with a silk tie hanging loose around his neck, as if he had been about to put it on when her assault on the doorbell had interrupted him. He was dark and young, that much registered before her mind hazed over again and she closed her eyes against the sickening wave of faintness.

'Don't you have a tongue in your head?'

Rowan felt herself being shaken, not hard, just

enough to make her try to gather her thoughts together.

'Who the hell *are* you? What are you doing here?'

'I. . .' Her dry throat made her voice croak painfully, and she tried desperately to swallow to relieve it. 'I need——'

'What is it? What's wrong?'

His tone had changed subtly, the angry impatience fading from it, and the new note of concern Rowan heard had her eyes flying open to look straight into a pair of deep grey ones, so dark that they were almost black, beautiful, stunning eyes that held her mesmerised, unable to look away.

I could fall in love with a man with eyes like that, she thought dreamily, breaking off on a cry of shock as she was shaken again, more roughly this time.

'Are you ill or crazy or what? You arrive on my doorstep—— Hey, steady!'

His voice sharpened as Rowan swayed on her feet, the movement making her wet black hair fall back from her face so that for the first time the long, ugly graze was exposed.

'Dear God, what happened to you?'

The sudden gentleness of the man's voice, the warm, supportive arm that came around her waist, were the last straw as far as Rowan was concerned. He seemed so strong and she was totally weak and lost. She lifted her hand in an uncertain, pleading gesture.

'Please,' she managed shakily, her voice just a thin thread of sound. 'Please help me.'

The effort of speaking exhausted her dwindling store of energy. There was a sound like the buzzing of a thousand angry bees in her ears, the world seemed to be spinning around her, and her last thought before she slipped into unconsciousness was the sudden realisation that what she had taken to be the sound of the doorbell going on and on, in spite of the fact that her hand no longer pressed it, was in fact the loud and insistent ringing of the telephone.

* * *

When Rowan finally woke she lay for a moment staring up at the ceiling, thinking herself back at home and the terrible events of the past days just an appalling dream.

She had learned her lesson, she thought drowsily. The first thing she would do when she got up would be to tell Bernard everything, admit what she had done and ask his forgiveness. He would listen—he had always been a very fair-minded man. Between them they could work out some way——

Her mind froze in mid-thought as she registered the fact that the light that filtered through the lace curtains at the window as not, as she had believed, the hazy sun of early morning, but that of the last hours of late afternoon. With a sharp cry she pulled herself up on the pillows and stared round her, her blue eyes wide with shock.

She was *not* at home. This room, with its thick carpet and heavy velvet curtains in a mellow shade of old gold, dark-wood fitted units and this wide double bed, was one she had never seen before. Her hands went to her face, the light touch making her flinch as it brushed against the raw graze at her temple, and a shivering wave of panic swept through her as memory came flooding back.

She was here, in that house. But *where* was here? What house was this—and who was the man who owned it?

She remembered him vividly—or rather she remembered those deep grey eyes that had probed hers so searchingly, making her feel that she could easily lose herself in their depths. She had woken a couple of times during the afternoon, she now realised, once as she recovered from her faint, before she had drifted into the heavy sleep of total exhaustion, and again when some small sound had disturbed her and she had surfaced hazily for just a few seconds, and each time her blurred gaze had opened on to those dark, watchful eyes, something in their expression relaxing her so that she had once more fallen asleep, her mind much more peaceful than it had been for days.

She had told herself that she could easily fall in love with such a man, she remembered, the recollection of that crazy, irrational feeling making her move restlessly under the bedclothes—a movement that stopped abruptly as the soft brush of fine linen against her skin brought home to her the fact that she was completely naked. How had she got here? Who had undressed her? Had *he*——?

The sudden opening of the bedroom door startled her, and in a flurry of panic she grabbed at the bedclothes, unnecessarily pulling them even closer around her.

'So you're awake at last.'

The deep voice was softer than she remembered; it had probably been shock at her dramatic arrival that had made it sound harsh before.

'I thought you were going to sleep the whole day away.'

'I—haven't been sleeping well lately.'

It was hard to get the words past the knot in her throat. Her heart was still beating wildly after her panic-stricken reaction to his sudden appearance, her discomposure aggravated by the knowledge that under the bedclothes she was completely naked—a fact that he, apparently, was well aware of. She had never felt so frighteningly vulnerable as she did now, alone with this man who was a complete stranger to her—unless it was on that morning, nearly two days ago, when Colin——

Her mind flinched away from that train of thought, and in order to distract herself from such painful memories she concentrated her attention on the man before her.

After the incredible impact of those amazing eyes, she might have found the rest of him a disappointment, but instead she found that he was an imposing-looking character, his face having a forceful power that went

far deeper than mere handsomeness. That lean, mus-
cular body was now clad in a white T-shirt and a pair
of close-fitting denim jeans that clung to a narrow waist
and hips and long, powerful thighs. What had happened to the elegant suit? Rowan could have sworn
that when he had opened the door he had been in the
process of dressing, on his way out—and probably to
somewhere very important, to judge by the impatience
in his tone.

The change of clothes gave him a very different
image from the man she had first seen. *He* had been a
sleekly sophisticated businessman, everything about
him declaring money, power and influence, even to
her fuddled brain. This man was much more relaxed,
more approachable—much more human altogether.

'And you haven't been eating well, either,' he was
saying now, moving to place the tray that he held on
the bedside table. 'You're painfully thin. I made some
soup and sandwiches—do you think you could sit up
and try to eat something?'

Rowan had moved automatically, beginning to ease
herself up on the pillows, before realisation struck
home and she grabbed at the blankets again, turning
wide, accusing blue eyes on his face.

'Did *you* undress me?'

'Of course.' He appeared quite unconcerned by her
vehemence, his voice calm and, to Rowan's mind,
infuriatingly indifferent.

'How. . .' She swallowed nervously as those deep
grey eyes swung round to her face. 'How dare you?'

'Dare?' Dark eyebrows lifted with a hint of mockery.
'Dare didn't come into it—and neither did any of the
perverted sexual feelings you're clearly thinking of
attributing to me. It was a practical move, pure and
simple—and one that was very necessary. You were
soaked through to the skin and dangerously cold. I had
to get you warm and dry as quickly as possible, and
putting you into bed seemed to be the most logical

move. I also bathed the cut on your face. Are you
going to object to that as well?'

'No.'

Ashamed and embarrassed, and feeling thoroughly
put in her place, Rowan lowered her eyes to stare
fixedly at her tightly clasped hands.

'I'm sorry—and I want to thank you for what you've
done. You've been very kind.'

She sensed rather than saw the shrug that dismissed
her stumbling apology—and her gratitude—as
unimportant.

'What else could I do? You appear on my doorstep,
hurt, distraught, and clearly very close to total col-
lapse. I just did what I thought was best. That
cut——' his tone had sharpened perceptibly '—what
happened to you?'

'I—fell.'

Rowan cursed the weak tears that sprang to her
eyes, hating the way they made her voice tremble. She
felt frighteningly lost and vulnerable, not knowing
what to say or do. How could she possibly answer if he
questioned her any further?

'I think we'll leave that for now; you're obviously
not up to answering questions. What you really need is
something to eat.'

Rowan nodded dumbly, intensely grateful for this
temporary reprieve. The soup smelled wonderful, and
already her stomach was growling inelegantly at the
thought of food. But sitting up meant exposing herself
to those probing grey eyes.

'Do you have something I could wear? I. . .' Her
hands moved in a fluttering, uncertain gesture, indicat-
ing her naked shoulders.

'There should be something. Hang on a sec—I'll go
and look.'

He was back amazingly quickly, well before she was
mentally ready, before she had had time to adjust to
her situation and think of what she was going to do—
or, more importantly, what she was going to *say*. Her

confusion was increased by the fact that in his hands was a pretty pink and white cotton robe that was very obviously feminine.

'My sister's,' he explained, seeing her surprised reaction. 'It should fit well enough—you're about the same size. Do you want any help?'

'*No!*'

Rowan's swift denial came out sharply, rosy colour washing her cheeks. It didn't matter that he had already seen her naked when he had undressed her— then she had been unconscious, oblivious to what had been happening to her. To expose herself knowingly to that narrow-eyed gaze was more than she could bear.

At least, seeing her obvious discomfort, he had the tact to turn his back while she struggled into the garment, not daring to get out of bed because of a distinct suspicion that her legs were still as weak as cotton wool and would not support her. But Rowan was very sure that, even though his attention was directed out of the window, he was well aware of every move she made, and one sign of weakness would have him turning back to her at once.

'All right,' she said at last, feeling rather better with the robe fastened securely round her. 'You can look now.'

An unfortunate turn of phrase, she realised, as he swung round, his eyes sweeping over her in a leisurely survey, a distinctly disturbing, sensual smile curling his lips.

'You have a very pretty body.' His voice was a silky drawl, one that raised goose-bumps of reaction all over Rowan's skin. 'There's no need to be ashamed of it.'

'I'm not ashamed!' Rowan declared hotly—too hotly, her tone very much at odds with her words. 'It's just that we're not. . .'

Her voice failed her as blue eyes locked with grey and she saw the way that sensual gleam still lingered in the darkness of his gaze.

'We're not very well acquainted,' she finished inanely, colour rushing to her cheeks as she heard his dry laughter.

'We're not acquainted at all. I don't even know your name.'

'It's Rowan—Rowan Carey.'

There was no danger in telling him that. After all, they were far enough away from Carborough for him never to have heard of her stepfather's firm, and even if he had he was unlikely to connect her with Bernard Stewart.

'And I'm Nathan Kennedy.'

'Nathan!' Rowan couldn't stop herself. Stress, hunger, and a devastating mental weakness had brought her to the verge of hysterical giggles. 'What do your friends call you? Nat?'

Her levity was a mistake; she knew that as soon as she saw the frown that darkened Nathan Kennedy's face.

'My *friends* call me Nathan,' he declared cuttingly, and Rowan felt all the warmth leave her body as intuition warned her that there was another, very different side to this man, one that the casual friendliness he had shown towards her so far had hidden until now. Every instinct warned her that she would be unwise to risk bringing that Nathan out into the open.

'I'm sorry,' she murmured hastily. 'Nathan it is, then——'

She was interrupted by a savage growling from her empty stomach, bringing a wash of embarrassed colour to her cheeks.

'I think it's time you ate something,' Nathan commented drily, picking up the soup bowl and holding it out to her. 'Here—and I want you to finish every last bit of it.'

His instructions were unnecessary. From the first spoonful, Rowan realised just how hungry she was, and the thick vegetable soup vanished rapidly, as did the chicken sandwiches that accompanied it. She was so absorbed that she didn't notice Nathan move to a chair and sit down, his hands clasped and his chin resting on them, dark, probing eyes studying her face intently.

'You *were* hungry,' he commented drily, as she finished and laid down the spoon with a contented sigh. 'When did you last eat?'

'I—I'm not sure. Breakfast yesterday, I think.'

'Yesterday?'

His tone alerted her, making her muscles tense in apprehension. He had been amazingly patient, holding back on the questions she knew must be burning in his mind, but now his patience was wearing thin and it showed in his voice.

'That was lovely—thank you,' she said hastily, leaning precariously out of the bed to replace the bowl on the bedside table in order to avoid looking into his face, feeling unable to meet those keen, watchful eyes. 'And now, if you'll just tell me what happened to my clothes, I'll get dressed and. . .' And what? She was still in exactly the same position as before. She had no money, no car, and no idea where she was or what she was going to do. She only knew that she couldn't stay here. She had imposed on Nathan enough, and unless she went quickly she would have to explain—and that was something she couldn't bring herself to do. 'I'll be on my way,' she concluded awkwardly.

'That's it?' Incredulity roughened Nathan's voice. 'It's been nice meeting you, goodbye?'

'I'm very grateful for everything you've done.' Rowan kept her eyes fixed on her hands, noting absently how they had clenched on the bedspread and forcing herself to make them relax; they revealed too much about her state of mind for comfort. 'And I'll pay for the soup. . .' With what? a near-hysterical part of her brain demanded. With the single tenpence piece that remained in her purse? Where *was* her purse? Automatically she glanced round the room. 'Where did I leave my handbag?'

'To hell with your handbag!' Nathan's violent explosion had her recoiling back against the pillows in fear. 'And to hell with the bloody soup! Do you think I give a damn about that? You turn up here out of the blue, obviously at the end of your tether——' He raked both hands roughly through his thick dark hair and got to his feet as if unable to sit still any longer. 'You ask for my help—*beg* for it—then pass out cold at my feet, and now you say you'll just get dressed and go on your way as if nothing had happened!'

'I—don't want to impose on you.' Rowan wished he hadn't stood up. He was too big, too imposing on his feet, making her feel intensely vulnerable and disturbingly aware of the fact that underneath the delicate cotton of the borrowed robe she was completely naked—as he very well knew. 'You've been so very kind, and I do appreciate it.' She was babbling uncontrollably, but she couldn't help it. Her nerves were so tightly stretched that she feared they might snap any moment. 'I'm very grateful to you for all your help, but you've done enough. I—I can't impose on you any longer,' she repeated with a touch of desperation.

'And what if I don't regard it as an imposition?'

The sudden switch in Nathan's tone from taut impatience to this soft question was a powerful shock, bringing Rowan's startled blue gaze to his face in a rush. As their eyes met and locked, Rowan felt as if her heart had stopped beating, as if she had ceased to breathe and were suspended in a timeless vacuum in which all she knew was that this man was somehow very special in a way she couldn't rationalise or attempt to explain.

That strongly moulded face gave such an initial impression of hardness, of a powerful confidence that came close to arrogance, but, looking closer, she saw the small lines around his mouth and eyes that spoke of frequent laughter and an easy, warm smile.

He wasn't smiling now, but there was something

about the way his eyes held hers that made it impossible to look away. He could be tough, she sensed intuitively, but he would always be honest and direct, with no pretence. He was the sort of man it wouldn't be easy to get to know, but the effort involved would be well worth it in the end.

But she wasn't going to have the chance to get to know him. They were just ships that passed in the night, two strangers who had met by accident and whose paths would now diverge, taking them in totally different directions so that they would never see each other again. Something twisted deep in her heart at the thought, and in her mind a small, lonely little voice cried that she didn't want to go, that more than anything she wished she could stay here, with Nathan.

'Rowan?' Nathan prompted quietly. 'Did you hear what I said?'

Still stunned by the revelations that her mind had opened to her, Rowan could only nod silently, unable to find the single syllable necessary to answer him.

'I——' Nathan began, then broke off abruptly, clearly thinking better of what he had been about to say. 'No—let me put it this way. Today has been a rather—difficult—time for me. Nothing has gone the way I planned it—and I don't just mean you arriving on the doorstep like that,' he added hastily, seeing the way Rowan bit her lower lip in consternation.

Rowan found the way he had noticed the tiny, betraying movement infinitely disturbing, revealing as it did just how closely he was watching her, noting every fleeting expression that crossed her face. Once again her hands tightened on the bedspread, even though she struggled to will them to relax.

'I never expected to be here tonight. I thought I'd be miles away, but because of—a change in plans—I *am* here and I don't particularly relish the prospect of being here on my own.' Nathan paused, rubbing one hand against his cheek in a gesture of disturbed thoughtfulness. 'You asked for my help, and if there's anything I can do——What I'm trying to say is that if it would help to have somewhere to stay tonight then you're welcome to a bed here.'

'Oh, Nathan!'

It was a shaken gasp, caught between delight and tears as Rowan fumbled for something to say. She had the crazy, impossible feeling that she had just been handed the world on a plate—but that gift was just a delusion, as much a mirage as the vision of an oasis in the desert that she had earlier thought Nathan's house to be. She couldn't accept Nathan's offer without admitting just why she had appeared on his doorstep so suddenly, and that was what destroyed her joy in his offer of help and brought hot, bitter tears to her eyes.

'Look——'

Nathan came to her side, sitting on the bed and capturing one of her tightly clenched hands in his, his touch warm and gentle, like a soothing balm to her bruised mind. Rowan was intensely aware of the strength of that hand, the broad expanse of his chest, the scent of his body, the sudden jerking of her heart bringing a dryness to her mouth so that she wetted her lips nervously with her tongue.

'Something's obviously wrong, and I'd like to help if I can. You're upset—you've been hurt.'

Dark, frowning eyes went to the graze on her face and Rowan had to blink furiously to force back the weak tears that were so perilously close as she saw the concern that sobered Nathan's expression. If she had wanted to stay before, she *longed* to do so now.

'So tell me—what happened?'

What happened? Two words guaranteed to freeze her tongue, throw her mind into a total, vacant blank so that she felt like some child's toy whose battery had just died, unable to think or move, knowing only the yearning desire to stay here, with Nathan, to stop running if only for this one night.

'Rowan?'

His soft use of her name was Rowan's undoing. A tear slid out of the corner of one eye and she ducked her head in embarrassment, afraid that Nathan would see it. But he *had* seen it, and a gentle hand slid under her chin, lifting her face towards his.

'I can't help if you won't tell me what's wrong.'

Perhaps she *could* tell him, Rowan thought, looking into his face to see the sympathy and solicitude that was stamped on it, softening his eyes until they were the hazy colour of mist. Perhaps he could help if he understood—if he knew the truth.

The truth. The words were like a slap in her face, jolting her out of the foolish, self-deluding reverie into which she had drifted. The truth was that she had behaved stupidly, irresponsibly and, ultimately, criminally. She had betrayed Bernard's trust in a way that would devastate her mother if it was to come out— *when* it came out, she amended painfully, recalling Colin's threats. In fact, Bernard and her mother must know already because, by now, Colin must have gone to them, told them everything.

'Rowan. . .'

Panic made Rowan feel as if her mind had blown a fuse as Nathan's gentle prompting pushed her to the edge of the precipice. How could she tell him when, inevitably, he would be as disgusted as her mother and stepfather must be?

She could imagine herself speaking the words, see in her mind the change that would come over his face. That caring, sympathetic light would fade from his eyes, the hand that held hers would be snatched away as his expression hardened against her. She could almost sense already the withdrawal that would follow her disclosure, a cold, numbing ache filling her as if it had already happened. The other Nathan Kennedy, the man she had glimpsed briefly earlier, would re-appear, burying *this* Nathan under an avalanche of contempt, and she would never get a chance to know him as she had wanted, because how could he want to know *her* when he had learned the truth?

'Rowan!' Nathan's voice had sharpened noticeably. 'What are you running away from? *Tell me!*'

With a despairing cry Rowan pulled her hands from under his and lifted them to cover her face, blotting out the sight of his face so very close to hers. But she couldn't blot out the truth; couldn't wipe out what she had done.

'Don't ask! I can't——! I can't tell you!'

'Why not?' Nathan pressed her inexorably. '*Why* can't you tell me?'

'Because it's—I——'

And suddenly it was as if something had exploded in her mind so that there was just a dazzling white light of inspiration that blinded her to everything else.

'I can't tell you what happened because I don't remember any of it!'

CHAPTER TWO

'I DON'T *remember*.'

Rowan heard her own voice speak the lie with a shock that made her mind reel. She *couldn't* have said that! How could she have said anything that was so appallingly, blatantly untrue?

But she *had* said it. Nathan's shocked silence told her that the words hadn't just been inside her head as she had heard them in that devastating moment of inspiration to which her desperation had driven her. She had said them and she couldn't go back on them now, unless she added the admission of the lie to all the other stupidities and failings she would have to admit to him. She was committed to that story, and, unless she wanted Nathan to recoil from her in disgust, probably throw her out of the house at once, she was going to have to stick to it—for tonight at least. Perhaps tomorrow, when she didn't feel so terribly tired, she might be able to think of some way out of it.

'I don't remember,' she whispered again from behind her concealing hands.

If she didn't have to look at his face, then perhaps she might not feel quite so terrible about what she had said. But how could she possibly feel any worse? Wasn't what she had done already bad enough without adding *this* to it?

'Rowan. . .'

Nathan's voice was husky and shaken, his evident disquiet stabbing like a knife into Rowan's guilty heart. She wished she could crawl under the bedclothes and hide. No, what she really wished was that the ground would open and swallow her up, taking her away from the shame and sense of self-disgust that assailed her now.

A choking cry of shock escaped her as she felt Nathan's hands on hers, easing her taut fingers away from her face. For a second Rowan struggled to resist the gentle pressure, then, knowing it was futile, abandoned the attempt and let him take her hands in his, though she closed her eyes against the sight of his face, knowing that the concern she would see there would be a bitter reproach to her.

'I didn't know—I never suspected.'

'How could you?' Sardonic flippancy gave her voice a brittle edge that she detested. How *could* Nathan have suspected something that didn't exist, something that was a lie through and through? 'It's not something that shows on the outside—like a bruise or a wound.'

And the wound in her heart didn't show either, she reflected miserably—and now she must never let it. It was self-inflicted and she deserved no sympathy at all for it from anyone, least of all herself.

'But you know your name.'

Oh, God, she'd forgotten that she'd told him that. But, of course, when she'd revealed her name she had had no idea of starting out on this tangle of lies that now seemed to grow around her like some huge, nightmarish spider's web, ensnaring her in its sticky coils.

'I—It was in my——' She had been about to say that her name was printed in her cheque-book, but, recalling that that particular item wasn't in her handbag—after all, she wouldn't be in this mess if it was—she hastily caught herself up and amended it to, 'My diary.'

Another wave of guilt swept through her as she saw Nathan nod acceptance of her words, growing to sickening proportions as she saw the way his eyes went to the graze on her face, a worried frown creasing his brow.

'So you must have knocked yourself out when you got that. And you've no idea what happened?'

Rowan didn't know if she shook her head in answer

to his question or in despair at what she had done. She knew exactly how the accident had happened, and she hadn't lost consciousness for a minute.

When her car had spluttered to a halt on the deserted moorland road she hadn't known which way to turn. The last village she had passed was miles away, and some sort of primitive fear of retracing her steps, going back to a place where someone might have noticed her and so could describe her if anyone—Colin, perhaps—came looking for her, had made her reluctant to head in that direction. *Would* it be Colin who would come looking for her? Or would it be Bernard—or even the police?

That fear had made her determined to go on—but in which direction? In desperation she had climbed to the top of a steep slope, looking for some landmark towards which she could make her way, but she had seen nothing. On every side the countryside had stretched out around her like some green and gold patchwork quilt, without any sign of a village or even a house to break it up, and so, in desperately low spirits, she had started to make her way back to the road. Halfway down the slope, with her mind on other things, she had missed her footing completely, slipped and fallen, tumbling all the way to the bottom and scraping her face on a stone in the process.

'I thought you'd just had some sort of fall.' The way Nathan's words picked up her thoughts was disturbing, aggravating her distress at hearing the note of self-reproach in his voice. 'But this changes everything. You could be badly concussed. I think you'd be better off in hospital.'

'*No!*' It was an instinctive reaction of pure, blind panic. Hospitals meant officials, forms, enquiries. Wouldn't that lead to the police being informed in case she had been reported missing? They would find out who she was, tell her mother, Bernard—and *Colin*. 'No, please, not a hospital!'

'Rowan.' The gentleness of Nathan's tone was meant

to be soothing, but instead it had quite the opposite effect, throwing her into a frenzy of alarm mixed painfully with self-reproach. 'You need medical attention. I could never forgive myself if you were badly hurt.'

'I'm not! Really, Nathan, I'm not! It's just that everything's—hazy. And you have nothing to reproach yourself for—you didn't know.' The last words caught in her throat, choking her.

'But I do now, and I can't just leave things like that. I have to be sure——'

'Oh, don't take me to a hospital—*please!*'

In desperation Rowan caught one of Nathan's hands in both her own, turning a pleading face towards him. She hated herself when she saw the confusion and doubt that clouded his eyes, cursing the way she had entangled him in the sordid mess she had made of her life—and he didn't even suspect that she had done it.

'Nathan, please! I don't know why.' Another lie, she thought despondently, feeling as if every untruth she had told were piling up around her like bricks fitting together to make a wall that before long would enclose her completely, cutting her off from the rest of the world. 'It's just that the thought of going into hospital terrifies me.'

'All right,' Nathan conceded slowly and with evident reluctance, 'if it worries you that much, we'll forget the hospital idea. But——'

He added that 'but' just as Rowan realised that she had been holding her breath and let it out in a sigh of relief, and immediately she tensed again in apprehension of what was coming.

'But I still want you checked over by a doctor. I'm going to ring George—George Lawrence. He's the local GP and a great friend of mine. He was going to be my best——' Once more Nathan seemed to reconsider what he had been about to say, and broke off sharply. 'I'll get him to come up here and have a look at you—check you over, make sure that everything's

OK,' he went on in a tone that brooked no further argument. 'Will you agree to that?'

'If you insist,' Rowan agreed reluctantly.

How could she say anything else? To resist further would only arouse Nathan's suspicions, make him think that she had something to hide. A doctor was under oath to preserve the confidentiality of his patients, wasn't he? And, after all, if she really *had* lost her memory wouldn't she be as determined as he was to seek medical help?

Dear God, how *would* she behave if she'd lost her memory? That flash of inspiration that had appeared to be the answer to all her problems now seemed to hang round her neck like some giant millstone.

'I think that's a very good idea,' she added hastily.

'It's the only possible idea—and I *do* insist,' Nathan declared adamantly, gently extricating his hands from hers, which only now did she realise were still tightly grasping his fingers, and levering himself up off the bed. 'I'll ring George now. He's not on duty tonight.'

A strange expression crossed his face as he spoke, one Rowan found impossible to interpret. It was almost as if he had some very personal, private reason for knowing just why the doctor would be off duty.

'It should only take him ten minutes or so to get here, and then we'll know exactly where things stand. You just relax and I'll be back in a minute.'

Relax? Rowan thought despairingly as she listened to Nathan's footsteps descending the stairs. What hope did she have of obeying Nathan's instructions? She had never felt so appallingly tense and nervous in her life— except perhaps in that dreadful moment when she had walked into her office to find Colin at her desk, the company account-books open before him.

Rowan shuddered violently as she recalled how she had frozen in the doorway, her mind thinking of flight, of dashing out of the room, out of the building and away—away from the consequences of her stupid, irresponsible actions, her *criminal* actions. Because it had been at that moment that the full truth of what she had done had come home to her. But her body had refused to obey the panic-stricken instructions her brain had screamed at it, her legs had felt like lead, she couldn't have moved if she'd tried, and so she had had to stand there, her heart beating frantically high up in her throat, until some faint sound she'd made had alerted Colin to her presence and he had lifted his head, his cold, light eyes, gleaming with mocking triumph, going straight to her ashen face.

'No!'

Rowan moaned the word out loud as she moved restlessly in the bed, wanting to block out the terrible memory. But she couldn't erase it from her mind. It had happened, and that was why she was here now, alone and afraid—and her foolish lie to Nathan could only make things ten times worse.

She couldn't stay here! She couldn't face Nathan again, couldn't look him in the face knowing what she had done, the nasty little story she was hiding behind that wall of lies. She had to get away.

How long would Nathan be on the phone? A few minutes? Longer? He would have to tell the doctor part of the story at least; he couldn't just announce that he wanted his friend to come over, urgently, without any explanation. If she could just find her clothes. . . Maybe there was another way out of the house—a back staircase, perhaps?

Moving with infinite care, so as not to make any betraying sounds, Rowan eased her feet out of the bed and on to the floor, standing up slowly and carefully, testing to see if her legs would support her. She still felt weak and unsure of her balance, but at least she was upright; though she doubted that she could move anywhere very fast. The journey across the thick, soft carpet seemed to take an age, but at last she reached the wardrobe, reaching out a hand to its sliding doors.

'What the hell do you think you're doing?'

The sharp question, coming so unexpectedly from

the doorway behind her, was like a physical blow, causing Rowan to spin round dangerously quickly, throwing herself off balance. With a shocked cry she threw out a despairing hand to stop herself falling, knowing it was already too late.

But she never hit the ground. In one swift movement Nathan was at her side and caught her in his arms, swinging her up off her feet with an ease that revealed the true strength of the muscles outlined by that clinging T-shirt. The next moment Rowan's shock and confusion vanished or, rather, changed to a form that was just as disturbing, but very different in origin.

The sensations she now experienced were those of a supremely physical awareness of the warmth of Nathan's body reaching her through the thin material of her robe, the powerful expanse of his chest and shoulders, the iron grip that held her. Nathan wore no aftershave or cologne, and the scent of his skin so close to hers was far more potent than any artificially created perfume.

It wasn't just weakness or exhaustion that was making her head spin, Rowan realised dazedly. It was the effect Nathan Kennedy was having on every one of her senses. Rowan was not inexperienced where men were concerned; without vanity she knew that her petite, dark looks were the sort that attracted male attention, and she had had no lack of escorts since she had been fifteen. But none of the men she had ever met had had this immediate, devastating impact that made her intensely aware of her own femininity, her body tingling with glorious, glowing sensation from head to toe.

And what about Nathan? Did he feel it too, this amazing sense of their difference and yet their unity, this recognition of his potent maleness and her femaleness? Held close against his chest as she was, she couldn't see his face as he strode across the room, carrying her towards the bed.

The force with which he deposited her on the gold-quilted bedspread was not the action of a man with passion in his mind, and one swift glance at his face had Rowan's heady euphoria evaporating like mist before the sun as she saw that the expression on it was one of controlled exasperation; the emotion that turned those dark eyes black as jet was anger, not desire. An overwhelming sense of loss assailed her, making her want to curl into a tight, defensive ball and bury her face in the pillows.

'I told you to stay where you were!'

Rowan flinched at the sound of Nathan's tone, recalling unwillingly that other, very different man she had sensed behind his easy charm a short time before.

'What in God's name were you doing out of bed?'

'I—was looking for my clothes.'

The loss of that wonderful intoxication made Rowan's voice tremble uncontrollably. She had thought she had felt lost and afraid before, but that had been as nothing when compared with her mood now. She felt totally bereft and terrifyingly vulnerable.

How could this man who appeared to feel nothing but irritation towards her spark off the sensual explosion she had experienced just moments before? And what good were those feelings if they weren't reciprocated? Such sensations should be shared, enjoyed, not bring this terrible, lonely emptiness in their wake.

'Your *clothes*?' Nathan's exclamation was an explosion of fury. 'Your clothes, little lady, should be the last thing on your mind right now. For one thing, you're not moving from that bed until George gives you the all-clear, and for another, I doubt if the things you had on will be at all wearable in the future. Your dress was completely ruined.'

'Oh, no—it can't be!' How could she ever leave here if she had nothing to wear?

Too late, Rowan realised that her outburst could be interpreted as a purely frivolous concern for her appearance, which was a bitter irony, because the truth was that she didn't give a damn about her dress and jacket—they, and almost every other outfit in her wardrobe, would be a physical reminder of the terrible thing she had done.

Guilt twisted in Rowan's heart as she recalled the way her mother's pale, thin face had lit up in delight at the sight of her daughter dressed in the sort of clothes she herself loved, but which now, being confined to a wheelchair, she never had a chance to wear. But Bernard had bought those clothes for her. He had indulged her every whim, treating her as the daughter he had never had—and how had she repaid him?

'I'll buy you another dress if that's what's worrying you.' Nathan's reaction confirmed her fears that what she had said could be misinterpreted.

'That isn't what I meant. I just——What am I going to wear when I leave here?'

'How many times do I have to tell you that you can't even think of leaving until George says you're all right? When that time comes, we'll find something for you to wear.'

A swift, searching glance swept over her, making her suddenly embarrassingly aware of the way the pink and white robe had been disturbed when he had carried her to the bed, its front pulled askew and now gaping revealingly over the curving white flesh of her breasts. Something in that dark-eyed gaze had her hands moving awkwardly to tug the two sides together, another aching sense of loss starting up inside her at the realisation that Nathan's scrutiny was purely objective, something that was confirmed by his next words.

'I'm sure something of Alexa's will fit you.'

Still, wasn't it better this way? Rowan told herself with stern realism. What possible hope could there be of any relationship between herself and Nathan when the lies she had told and the things she had done must always come between them? And the last thing she needed right now was any involvement with any man. In her loneliness and fear, she was reacting instinctively to her inner need to have someone help and protect her, her brain not functioning properly as a result of shock. She must be on her guard against rushing in where angels feared to tread. She had given her trust too quickly in the past, and look where that had got her.

'One thing. . .'

A new note in Nathan's voice alerted Rowan to the fact that what he was about to say was something very different from his casual remark about finding her something to wear, and with an effort she dragged her thoughts out of the swamp of misery into which they had fallen and forced herself to concentrate on what he was saying.

'Your clothes—they were all very good quality, expensive, stylish. Whoever you are, you're not exactly impoverished.'

He meant it to be encouraging, a tiny clue to the person he believed she had lost as a result of her fall. Perhaps he hoped it would excite her, intrigue her, make her think—which it did, but not in the way Nathan had intended.

Rowan had to bite down hard on her lower lip to keep back the unthinking words that had almost escaped her. She knew her clothes were good, knew exactly how much Bernard had paid for them, and that fact was another stabbing reproach at the thought of how her stepfather had always loved to spoil her. But that had been in the days when the firm had been in a much better shape. Just lately things had been going downhill rapidly—and now she had aggravated Bernard's problems, making things even worse.

'The label in that dress is pretty exclusive. That shop has only one or two branches up north, so I'm sure if we tracked them down we'd have a chance of finding some clue to where you live, at least.'

Through the cold, creeping fear that his words provoked Rowan suddenly felt a new and previously unconsidered question take root in her mind.

'How come you know so much about women's clothes?'

Had that knowledge come from the sister he had mentioned, or—Rowan's eyes went to the long hands resting lightly on Nathan's narrow hips.

'Are you——?'

He had seen the movement and anticipated her question, and there was a sudden, inexplicable twist to his mouth as he answered.

'No, I'm not married. I was going to be, but—things changed.'

Downstairs, the sound of the doorbell cut into his words.

'That'll be George.' Nathan appeared almost relieved at his friend's arrival, as if it had spared him some explanation that he would have found difficult. 'I'd better go and let him in.'

Left alone, Rowan lay back against the pillows, trying to absorb all that had happened. Rationally, she knew she should be considering what she was going to say to the doctor, how she would answer his questions, but her mind refused to focus on such matters. All she could think about was Nathan.

Who *was* Nathan Kennedy? She was here, in his house, possibly even in his bed; she had put herself in his hands, lied in order to stay with him just a few short hours longer, and yet she knew nothing about him.

Mentally Rowan reviewed the few facts she had gleaned about her rescuer. He was wealthy—this house proved that. He had a sister—what had he said her name was? Alexa. So, was Alexa Kennedy older or younger than her brother? Rowan would guess that Nathan himself was thirty or thereabouts, possibly older, but he was unlikely to be any younger. No one acquired that instinctive air of command and control that he bore with the ease of a comfortable, well-worn jacket without some experience of life. He was a man in the prime of life, strong, attractive, with money to spare, so he was obviously well established in whatever career he had chosen—but he wasn't married.

Rowan recalled Nathan's reaction when he had realised that she had been about to ask him if he had a wife. She could picture his face vividly in her mind, the cynical way his mouth had twisted, the swift narrowing of his eyes. She could hear his words, 'I was going to be, but—things changed.' What had changed? Had his fiancée backed out, or had Nathan?

The sound of voices and the footsteps of the two men coming upstairs had her closing her mind off from that train of thought hastily, as if she feared that Nathan might be able to read her mind as he came into the room.

George Lawrence was a tall, well-built man with curly hair several shades lighter than Nathan's and touched with a hint of reddish copper. His blue eyes were clear and intelligent, his face less strongly carved than his friend's, giving him an open, sympathetic look that Rowan was willing to bet made him a favourite with his patients.

'Well, now, young lady, what happened to you?'

'I—don't know.'

Rowan had thought that with each repetition the lie would become easier to tell, familiarity breeding an indifference she could handle, but in fact the truth was quite the opposite. The deceitful words seemed to grow, sticking in her throat, and making her voice thick and rough.

'Some sort of accident, was it? Nathan said you'd told him you'd had a fall. Do you know how that happened?'

'I don't remember. It was just a guess when I said I'd fallen.'

She had forgotten that she'd told Nathan that. Was there anything else she'd said that cast doubt on her claim to have lost her memory? She didn't think so, but she couldn't be sure. Oh, *why* had she ever started out on this fraud?

Because she couldn't admit to the truth, that was why. But it was going to be so very hard to keep up the pretence. For all his quiet, gentle bedside manner, George Lawrence didn't look as if he were going to miss a trick—and now she had his medical knowledge to contend with. Just how many times could she say, 'I don't remember'?

'I don't think it can have been a very bad fall,' she added hastily, wanting to cover her tracks as much as possible. 'After all, there are no bones broken.'

'Hmm, well, you'd better let me be the judge of that. I'll need to give you a thorough examination just to be sure—if you don't mind waiting downstairs, Nathan,' he said with what Rowan, now perilously close to hysteria, thought was a totally unnecessary degree of tact considering the fact that his friend had been the one to undress her and put her to bed—or perhaps that was something Nathan had neglected to tell him.

'Sure.'

As Nathan turned towards the door Rowan felt as if a lifeline she had grasped was slipping from her hands. She didn't want him to go, couldn't bear to be left alone to answer George's questions.

'Nathan!'

Hearing her cry, he swung back, his eyes going to her face, a faint frown drawing his dark brows together.

'It's all right, Rowan,' he said quietly. 'You're in very good hands—and I'll just be downstairs.'

And with that Rowan had to be content, but as the door closed behind Nathan once again she experienced that devastating sense of loss and loneliness that had assailed her before.

In the end, the examination wasn't the ordeal that Rowan had dreaded. George was gentle, sympathetic, the perfect doctor, keeping strictly to the matter in hand, his questions not the personal ones she had feared, but concerned only with whether she could move her head easily, whether this hurt—or that—and Rowan was intensely grateful for that because her mind seemed to have lost its bearings, unable to concentrate on what was happening to her, instead drifting off into the realms of heated fantasy.

As she submitted to the doctor's professional, impersonal examination she found that her thoughts would keep wandering, imagining how differently she would feel if it had been Nathan's hands touching her in this way, Nathan's eyes on her, his voice asking those questions. The sensations those thoughts aroused were so disturbing that her blood warmed in her veins, washing her body with a rosy glow that she was sure would convince George that she was running a temperature, if not a raging fever.

'Well, you've been lucky,' George pronounced at last, his examination finished, and thankfully Rowan fastened the pink and white robe firmly round her again, concealing the betraying colour of her skin. 'Nothing more than a few bruises, and that cut on your face which isn't deep and should heal quite easily. You'll probably be pretty stiff in the morning, but it'll soon wear off. There's nothing there to worry about.'

She could have told him that, Rowan thought, relaxing back against the pillows. That tumble down the hill had been unlikely to cause any serious injuries. But George's next words drove away her sense of relief.

'What does concern me, though, is this loss of memory. You must have knocked your head pretty hard for that to happen. Really, what I'd like is to take you into Farmworth General for a head X-ray.'

'Oh, no—please—I——'

'Nathan said the idea scared you. What is it? Do you have some sort of phobia about hospitals?'

Rowan had opened her mouth to answer—but whether to say yes or no, she wasn't sure—when realisation struck home fast, reminding her that to admit to anything would reveal that she did know *something* about herself, that her past was not, as she had claimed, a complete blank.

'I don't know. But please don't make me go to hospital. I'm frightened.' Rowan caught a glimpse of herself in the mirror as she leaned forward pleadingly, and she couldn't help admitting that, although she knew all too well that she wasn't ill, she certainly looked the part. Her almond-shaped blue eyes were wide and over-bright, her thin face ashen except high on the delicate cheekbones where two patches of hectic colour burned fiercely.

'Now don't upset yourself.'

George came to sit on the bed beside her, taking her hand in his just as Nathan had done a short time before. But it wasn't the same, Rowan thought dazedly; not at all the same. For all he was an undeniably good-looking man, George was just a kindly doctor, his hand on hers as impersonal as his examination had been. It aroused no worrying yearning inside her, no glorious, heady intoxication, no aching need. She was aware only of his wish to comfort her, his kindness. When Nathan had sat beside her in this way, and again when he had picked her up and carried her to the bed, she had been intensely, searingly aware of him as a *man*.

'Seeing as it disturbs you so much, I'm going to go against my better judgement and leave you here for the night. You've had something of a shock; rest and quiet is what you need. In fact, it might be all that's necessary. You could well wake up tomorrow and remember everything.'

She certainly would, Rowan thought bitterly. Contrary to established belief, in the morning things would not look very much better; they were more likely to look very much worse. Tomorrow morning and for every other morning to come she would have to live with what she had done. Hot tears of shame and despair stung her eyes and she ducked her head to hide them.

'You needn't have any fears about Nathan.' George had misinterpreted the reasons for her distress. 'He's a great guy—straight as they come. You'll be quite safe with him.'

Rowan caught in her breath on a small, shocked gasp. Illogically, and possibly very foolishly, it had never occurred to her to wonder if she would be safe alone in this house with Nathan. Past events should have taught her that she was no great judge of character, rushing into trust with a dangerous speed. After all, she knew nothing at all about Nathan Kennedy.

'Who—who is Nathan?' she asked stumblingly.

'Nathan?' George had got to his feet and was searching in his case for something. 'Like I said, he's a great guy—my best friend, in fact. I've known him for years—we were at school together.'

'What does he do?'

'He's in the building trade.' George grinned suddenly. 'Though that's rather an understatement for the size of his operations. He owns Kennedy Construction—does that ring a bell?' he questioned sharply, hearing Rowan's swift intake of breath.

It rang hundreds of them, like a warning peal in her mind.

'No—nothing.' Rowan's response came swiftly, rather too swiftly perhaps, from someone who wasn't supposed to remember anything about herself, but she was beyond caring. George's revelation about Nathan's position had shaken her precarious grip on her self-control.

Kennedy Construction. Nathan was *that* Kennedy! Rowan hadn't worked in her stepfather's small building firm for four years without hearing of Kennedy Construction. Started by Alexander Kennedy, who must have been Nathan's grandfather, it was one of the major forces in the construction business in the whole country, and its owner and managing director had the prestige and influence in that field that the American Kennedys had had in politics.

A shiver ran down Rowan's spine at the thought of what might have happened if she had told Nathan more about herself at the beginning. Her stepfather's firm might be a tiny, Midland-based family business, but a Kennedy of Kennedy Construction could well know about it—in fact, she was sure that they would make it their policy to know. Kennedy Construction was well known for its interest in small firms that might be worth buying up and absorbing into their massive corporation—and Nathan was Kennedy Construction. Knowing that, how could she stay here now?

'I don't think—perhaps it would be best if——' Try as she might, Rowan couldn't make the words form a coherent pattern in her mind so that she could say anything clearly.

'Now calm down, or I'll reconsider my decision not to admit you to hospital.'

Hospital—Nathan *Kennedy*—which was the lesser danger? Rowan didn't know, and couldn't gather her scattered thoughts to consider the problem.

'Now——' George turned, a small syringe in one hand '—you've had a considerable shock and you're obviously shaken and under stress. I'm going to give you a mild sedative—something to help you sleep—and then we'll see how you are in the morning.'

'But Nathan——'

'But Nathan, nothing.' The quiet, firm voice drew Rowan's eyes to the doorway immediately. She had only heard perhaps a few hundred words in those attractive, faintly husky tones, but already they seemed as familiar to her as her own. 'Just do as George says, Rowan. We can talk about everything in the morning when you're rested.'

Everything. Rowan echoed the word bitterly in her mind. There was nothing they could talk about, nothing she could tell him, because anything she said would only drive him away from her. In her misery she scarcely felt the prick of the needle as George administered the sedative.

'Is she OK?' she heard Nathan ask.

'Fine. A few bumps and bruises, but otherwise nothing to worry about—apart from the amnesia, of course, but that——' He broke off abruptly, and when he spoke again Rowan had the distinct impression that his words were not the ones he had originally intended. 'That we'll have to leave to time to heal. What this young lady needs most of all is sleep.'

'You heard what the doctor said.' Nathan had crossed to the side of the bed and pulled the blankets up around Rowan's shoulders. 'Settle down now, and don't worry about a thing. I'll keep an eye on you. My room's just next door, so if you wake in the night and want anything you only have to call—I'm a very light sleeper.'

She would never be able to sleep, Rowan reflected miserably, not with the burden of guilt and worry that hung round her neck like an iron weight. But she had no alternative but to obey Nathan's instructions and, with a sigh, she settled back against the pillows. It was going to be a long, dark, lonely night.

'You'll call again in the morning?' Nathan asked George.

'I'll be here as soon as early surgery's finished,' his friend agreed. 'Don't let her out of bed until then.' He snapped the clasp of his case shut and swung it off the table. 'How are things with you?' he asked, his voice so low that Rowan had to strain to hear it.

Nathan's shoulders lifted in a dismissive shrug. 'How do you think? All in all, it's been one hell of a day, what with Meryl—and now this.'

Meryl? Rowan wondered hazily. She could have sworn that Nathan had said that his sister's name was Alexa—and Alexa fitted better, now that she knew just who Nathan was. She would be named after her grandfather—the founder of Kennedy Construction. That thought had her moving restlessly in the bed, drawing both men's eyes to her.

'Relax,' George soothed. 'That sedative should start to work soon.'

Surveying Rowan's white, drawn face, shocking against the intense black of her hair, he frowned.

'I'd like to talk to you, Nathan,' he said. 'Downstairs, perhaps?'

'Sure,' Nathan agreed easily. 'How about a drink before you go? I've made some fresh coffee. I'd offer you something stronger if you weren't driving—I think I could do with a drink myself.'

George had been right, the sedative *was* beginning to work and Rowan was starting to feel pleasantly drowsy, but she was still awake enough to catch the expression on Nathan's face, a flash of apprehension and fear searing through the cotton-wool effect in her mind as she recognised it as being strongly reminiscent of the one that had been there when he had told her that he had been going to get married, but that something had prevented it.

'There's plenty of champagne.' It wasn't the effects of the drug, she *had* heard the dark, bitterly satirical note in his voice. 'I reckon I'll be drinking the stuff for months.'

Through heavy lids, Rowan saw the hand George laid on his friend's arm, the gesture of sympathy and understanding unmistakable. There was something wrong here, something she didn't understand, but every instinct told her that it wasn't just to do with her own intrusion into Nathan's life.

'Nathan?' she murmured sleepily.

'Hush, Rowan.' For a second Nathan's hand rested on her head, ruffling her hair gently in a way that, to her bitter disappointment, even her fogged brain couldn't describe as anything other than brotherly. 'It's time you were asleep.'

He wanted her asleep, Rowan thought. Wanted her quiet and out of his way so that he could get on with his own life and whatever was troubling him. If she had needed any further evidence of the fact that the heightened sensitivity that had shaken her hadn't touched him at all, then that careless caress would have convinced her. But she didn't need any proof. She knew that to Nathan she was just someone who needed help, someone he had taken pity on as he might have let a stray dog into his house on a cold, wet night.

'Try not to think about anything,' George added. 'You're in good hands here; Nathan will take care of you.'

'My friends call me Nathan.' Nathan's words, with that subtle emphasis on the *friends*, echoed in Rowan's clouded brain as the two men walked towards the door. My *friends*. There was nothing she wanted more than to be able to hope that, one day, Nathan Kennedy would count her among that special group he called his friends—or more. But how could that ever be? She couldn't pretend to have lost her memory for the rest of her life. Some time, and probably sooner rather than later, Nathan must find out what she had done, and when he did then surely the man George had described as 'straight as they come' would reject her completely?

CHAPTER THREE

'AND how are you feeling this morning?'

Guilt made her hypersensitive, Rowan reflected unhappily. She couldn't take Nathan's question at face value because behind it she could hear the unspoken queries he was holding back: Have you remembered anything? Who *are* you?

'I'm fine.'

An unwary move as she struggled to sit up made her wince.

'Ouch! Dr Lawrence wasn't joking when he said I'd be stiff when I woke up. I feel as if I'm black and blue all over.'

She regretted her flippancy immediately because it brought Nathan's eyes to her, lingering on the soft flesh exposed at the neck of her robe; regretted it because the look he gave her had none of the sensual warmth he had displayed so briefly the day before, but was as clinically objective as any examination George Lawrence might have made.

'You look quite normal to me. Much better than yesterday, anyway. Did you sleep well?'

'Like a log. That sedative the doctor gave me put me out like a light.'

And that was something for which she was intensely grateful. Without the injection, she was sure that she would have spent long, long hours lying awake with nothing to do but think—and thinking was definitely not her favourite occupation right now.

'Then you'll be ready for something to eat. Breakfast is served.'

Nathan laid a tray across Rowan's knees, the movement bringing him so close that she felt the soft brush of his hair across her cheek, the scent of his body reaching her nostrils and setting her pulse racing in an uncomfortable, jerky rhythm.

'And I want it all eaten—no argument. George said you were far too thin.'

Nathan had said that, too. Was that why he felt no attraction towards her? It was true that she'd hardly eaten a thing over the last couple of days, and before that just sitting opposite Colin at the table had driven her appetite away completely on occasions. Her mother had noticed, of course, Rowan thought on a pang of distress at the thought of the anxiety she had caused, particularly at a time when her mother needed to be protected from worry.

But now that worry would be so very much greater. Rowan surveyed the tray laden with fruit juice, coffee, scrambled eggs and toast, guilt closing her throat so that she was sure she wouldn't be able to swallow a single mouthful.

'After all, I don't want my hard work to go to waste.' Clearly Nathan had seen her dubious expression.

'*You* cooked this?'

Rowan couldn't hide her surprise. After seeing the size of the house, and the discovery that Nathan was the owner of Kennedy Construction, she had assumed that there would be a staff of some sort to help run the place—a housekeeper at least.

'Who do you think?'

A gleam of dry humour lightened those dark grey eyes in a way that, to Rowan, was far too appealing— dangerously so for her peace of mind.

'Well—a cook, or your sister.'

What had she said to drive the amusement from his eyes, the gleam fading like a candle suddenly extinguished in the wind? With a *frisson* of unease Rowan recognised that the other Nathan Kennedy, the one she feared, was back.

'Alexa's staying with friends and I gave the housekeeper the week off.' There was a distinct bite in Nathan's voice. 'I—wanted to be alone for a while.'

And that was a remark guaranteed to make Rowan
feel even worse than ever—if such a thing were possible. He had wanted to have some time on his own—
was that just in order to have a break from the
pressures of running Kennedy Construction, or did it
have something to do with the scene she had witnessed
last night and not understood? Another memory
drifted to the surface of her mind, that of Nathan
telling her that he had originally planned to be miles
away from home yesterday, but that things hadn't
worked out. Had he had some holiday plans that had
had to be cancelled at the last moment? Whatever the
reason, he had wanted to be alone and she had
intruded on his privacy.

'I'm sorry.'

'It's nothing to do with you,' Nathan told her curtly.
'Don't start feeling guilty; you couldn't help having an
accident. I'm just glad I was here to help. Now eat that
breakfast!'

With a hand that was noticeably unsteady, Rowan
reached for the glass of orange juice as Nathan lowered
himself into a chair, clearly intending to stay until she
carried out his instructions. That only increased her
conviction that she was going to find eating extremely
difficult. If she could moisten her dry throat, then
perhaps she could manage something, though she
would have found it much easier without him there,
lounging back in his chair with an indolent ease that
was belied by the keen, grey-eyed gaze fixed on her
face. How long would it be before his patience wore
thin and the questions began again?

She would have felt better if she had known that
there was someone else in the house. Not as a chap-
eron—she still felt intuitively that she had nothing to
fear from Nathan, and his evident indifference to her,
sexually at least, certainly seemed to confirm that fact.
But another person, particularly another female, might
have defused the situation, diluting the impact Nathan
had on her and so making it easier for her to cope.

'If you feel strong enough you can get up later on—
but not until George has had a look at you,' Nathan
remarked, his easy, conversational tone in such contrast to the tightly strung state of Rowan's nerves that
it brought a strong sense of unreality to the situation.
'We'll find something in Alexa's wardrobe to fit you,
and you can sit out in the garden. It's going to be a
beautiful, warm day, not at all like yesterday.'

'I'd like that.' Rowan was making slow headway
with her meal. Rationally, she knew she was hungry,
but her stomach was churning so much that she was
afraid it would reject the food she was forcing on it. 'I
don't think I can manage any more of this.' She
expected his frown, knew that the small amount she
had eaten wouldn't satisfy him.

'You can do better than that. You need to build
your strength up—I don't want you fainting on me
again.'

'I can't——'

'Come on, Rowan.' The soft, cajoling note that had
slipped into Nathan's voice was like a warm caress
across her skin. '*Try.*'

How could she resist the appeal of his voice, the
smile that encouraged and persuaded? Suddenly
Rowan knew she would do anything to please him,
anything to earn that smile again. The tension that had
gripped her slipped away, and she returned to the meal
with a new enthusiasm.

'That's better,' Nathan said approvingly when the
plates were empty and he had removed the tray. 'More
coffee?'

'Please.'

Rowan was amazed at how easy it had been to finish
the meal after all. And Nathan had been right, she did
feel better, stronger and much more relaxed. With a
contented sigh she leaned back against the pillows,
letting her eyes follow his movements as he poured the
coffee into her mug. He was once again dressed
casually in a pale yellow short-sleeved shirt and beige

jeans, the soft colour of the shirt throwing the deep brown of his hair into sharp relief. *This* Nathan she could be comfortable with, he raised no thoughts of the expensively tailored business man who had opened the door to her, the man she now knew as Nathan Kennedy, owner and managing director of Kennedy Construction.

Suddenly she became aware of the fact that Nathan had spoken again and she hadn't caught the single word he had used on a note of enquiry.

'I'm sorry—what did you say?'

He *couldn't* have said what she thought. Please God, let her have misheard him! But her prayers went unanswered.

'Carborough,' Nathan repeated clearly and firmly, swinging round to face her.

The explosion of panic in Rowan's mind made her head reel sickeningly. How did Nathan know the name of her home town? It couldn't be just a lucky guess, so where had he got his information from?

'I—don't understand. What do you mean?'

She was terrifyingly aware of those dark, probing eyes fixed on her face, so black and hard they looked as if they had been carved from jet.

'Carborough,' Nathan said again. 'It's a small town some miles from Birmingham. Does the name mean anything to you?'

It meant everything, so much so that Rowan couldn't think straight.

'No—I—why should it?'

'Because it's where you live.'

The cool, crisp words fell like ice against her sensitised nerves.

'Where I——?'

'Rowan Carey, 18 Oak Lane, Carborough.' Nathan's hand went to his pocket and pulled out a small, grey-backed notebook. 'It's all in here.'

With a shock that was like a blow to her heart, Rowan recognised her own diary and now, too late, she remembered how she had told him that she knew her name because it had been written in it.

'My diary!' Hastily she switched to aggression to hide her fear. 'You've been through my handbag!'

'I was trying to help,' Nathan put in quietly, but Rowan was beyond heeding him.

'How dare you pry into my things? You had no right!'

'Rowan——'

'What were you doing? Checking to see if I was telling the truth?'

'It wasn't like that at all. I thought that if there was a name in your diary, there was bound to be an address there too, and perhaps a telephone number—someone I could contact.'

'*Someone I could contact*.' Dear God, had he already rung Bernard, heard the whole story?

'You haven't. . .?' Rowan's voice failed her as she tried to frame the question. 'You haven't——?'

'No.'

The single syllable brought such a rush of relief that she sagged back against the pillows, limp with release from the tension that had held every muscle taut.

'I haven't phoned anyone. I wanted to check with you first.'

Nathan's eyes narrowed suddenly, that dark grey gaze sharpening as if he was trying to probe deep into her mind, read her innermost thoughts.

'Why does that worry you so much, Rowan? What are you afraid of?'

Colin—the truth—you—the answers buzzed inside Rowan's head, but she knew she couldn't admit to a single one of them. With a desperate struggle she got a grip on the shattered remnants of her self-control and forced herself to think logically. She was supposed to have lost her memory.

'Put yourself in my place.' Her voice was shaken and weak, but at least it had lost that shrill edge of panic that gave so much away. 'If all you knew about yourself

was your name and—and an address in a diary—would
you want to rush into contacting someone you didn't
remember? If, of course, there is anyone else there,'
she added hastily, realising that perhaps the implied
assumption that there would be someone at her home
address could be interpreted as *knowing* that. 'How
would you feel if someone claimed you as their
daughter——?'

Stepdaughter, her brain threw at her, making her
voice fail completely, and she had to swallow hard
before forcing herself to go on to fill the silence that
Nathan clearly had no intention of breaking. 'Or sister,
or flatmate, or whatever—and you didn't *know* them?'

'Don't you want to find out about yourself?'

'Yes, of course I do—but not like this, not so
suddenly. I haven't adjusted to what's happened. I'm
not ready to face anyone.'

And that at least was true, though not in the way
Nathan believed. The wall of lies was growing steadily
all the time, imprisoning her behind it.

'I need time, Nathan, time to adjust, to prepare
myself.' The stern, thoughtful set of Nathan's face gave
her no help or encouragement. She couldn't tell what
was going on in his mind, and his lids hooded his eyes,
hiding their expression from her. 'When I found my
name in that diary, of course I found the address too—
but I felt that I couldn't just ring up and announce that
I was Rowan.' More lies; more bricks. The wall was
getting higher and stronger with every word she spoke.
Would she ever be able to escape from it? 'After all, I
had no way of knowing that the handbag was even
mine.'

'It seems a logical assumption.'

'Yes,' Rowan agreed wearily, because there was
nothing else she could do. 'It is the logical assumption,
and I think it's the right one. I think I *am* Rowan
Carey, and there probably is someone at that address
who will know me, but I can't face them yet.'

'And what about them? What about the family,

friends——' Nathan's voice altered subtly '—a lover, perhaps? People who will miss you. How do you think they're feeling if you've just disappeared?'

Damn him! Rowan flinched as Nathan unerringly put his finger on one of the most painful aspects of her situation. How *was* her mother feeling? And Bernard? One thing was sure, there was no lover who would worry about her. Roy wouldn't even spare her a thought. Rowan felt a wave of intense relief wash over her, thanking God that at least she and Roy had never actually been lovers. How would she have felt then?

'I know.' It was a low moan of distress. 'Do you think I haven't considered that side of things? But I don't know what to do. I'm——' Ironically, her voice broke on the one really truthful statement she had made; the one which should have sounded confident and sure. 'I'm *scared!*'

'Oh, Rowan!'

She knew by Nathan's tone that she had won, but it was the most devastatingly hollow victory. She could feel nothing, not even a sense of relief as she saw his face lose that stern rigidity and take on an expression of gentle sympathy.

'I understand. I was pushing you too hard too soon— I'm sorry.'

'Don't!' Rowan choked, her voice thick with the tears that threatened to spill out on to her cheeks. 'Oh, please don't apologise!'

'But I feel I have to.' Once more Nathan came to sit beside her on the bed and, as on the previous night, would have taken her hands in his if she hadn't lifted them to cover her face and hide her tear-bright eyes, unable to cope with the thought of that physical contact.

'I shouldn't have done that. I should have realised how upset you'd be, especially when George said——'

The abrupt way he broke off, his sudden silence, drove Rowan to lower her concealing hands and look into his face in fearful apprehension.

'When George said what? Nathan—*what* did George say?'

'We had a long talk about amnesia and its possible causes.' Nathan's response came so slowly that Rowan had to bite down hard on her lower lip to stop herself from screaming at him to hurry up, tell her just what the doctor had said. 'Loss of memory isn't as common as popular novels would have us believe. Concussion *can* cause it, though it's more common to find that the patient doesn't remember the events leading up to the injury, while earlier memories aren't affected and can be recalled perfectly. The other sort——' Once more Nathan broke off, studying Rowan's face as if checking to assure himself that she could accept what he was going to say.

'The other sort?' Rowan prompted shakily, though it was not at all wha she wanted to say. What she really wanted to do was to tell him to stop, right now, because she was sure she wasn't going to like what he said.

Nathan ran a hand over his hair and sighed. 'The other form of amnesia is—to quote George—"nearly always a form of acute neurosis".' The sudden narrowing of Nathan's eyes showed that he had caught Rowan's involuntarily indrawn breath, but he continued clearly and firmly. 'Sufferers may "forget" their names, where they live and so on, but in fact the memory is suppressed, not lost.' Another of those keen, searching glances took in her pale face, her tensely held body, the tightly clasped hands lying in her lap. Rowan swallowed hard.

'Go on,' she croaked. 'I'm sure he told you more.'

Nathan nodded slowly, his expression sombre. The deep grey eyes were like dark, shadowy pools, no light showing in them at all. 'That sort of loss of memory is the result of some severe emotional shock, something that is more than the patient can bear to remember.'

'And you think that that is what's happened to me?'

Rowan was amazed at how even her voice sounded when in fact her mind was in turmoil. How did the

things Nathan had said affect her? What should she
say in answer to them? She had been the victim of the
popular misconception that a head injury could cause
complete loss of memory, and had seized on that fact
as her salvation in a moment of desperation. Now it
seemed that she had blundered into something much
deeper than she had anticipated, and she didn't know
how to handle it. She had pretended not to remember
in order to avoid dangerous questions about her past,
her background, but, according to George, that was
exactly what he and Nathan would now be most
concerned with; wanting to know what dark secret had
brought her to this condition. She might just as well
have told them that she had something to hide.

'I don't know what to think. George is the medical
man, but he admits he's no ex rt on this sort of thing.
It's not what you usually come up against in a small-
town practice.' A brief grin broke the tension in
Nathan's face. 'Measles and mumps are more in his
line.'

Rowan could find no answering smile in response to
his attempt to lighten the situation. 'Acute neurosis'. . .'Some severe emotional shock.' She felt as if
she had experienced that, all right, but her memory
was still as firm and clear as ever—frighteningly so.
Right now she wished with all her heart that her fake
loss of memory was in fact very real. She would give
the world not to have to remember.

'Can you still remember nothing at all?' Nathan
asked when she remained locked in her disturbed
thoughts.

How did she answer that? If she said no then,
logically, he would pursue the psychological theory
and try to find out just what trauma in her past had
created this situation—which was just the sort of
enquiry she most wanted to avoid. She could claim
that there were some beginnings of memory—vague
and unformed as yet—but would that be enough to

satisfy him, and wouldn't it seem rather suspicious, coming so soon after what he had said?

'I——' she began, not knowing what answer she could give, but at that moment, to her overwhelming relief, the sound of the doorbell broke in on her.

Nathan got to his feet. 'That'll be George. We'll see what he has to say before we take things any further.'

Left to herself, Rowan reviewed their conversation with a mind numbed by shock. In desperation the previous night she had seen her chance and grabbed it, never considering the possible consequences of her actions, but now those consequences were reaching out to enclose her like snaky tendrils of thorny bramble, and she couldn't shake them off. Thinking got her nowhere; she just seemed to be going round and round like someone caught in a large, dark maze, always coming back to the same point in the end, and as a result she was in a state bordering on hysteria by the time Nathan came back into the room with George at his side.

'Nathan tells me you think I'm neurotic.'

As a feeble attempt at a joke it fell painfully flat, the tightness in her throat making her voice come out shrill and accusing and very, very defensive.

'Not neurotic, Rowan,' Nathan corrected sharply. 'All I said was that your amnesia could be the result of some shock that was too much for you to cope with. We all have our breaking-points—it's just that some of us take longer to get there.'

'Do you still remember nothing?' George put in.

'No details,' Rowan managed uneasily. 'Not who I am or who my family are—nothing since I had to leave my car and started walking——'

'Your *car*?' Nathan pounced on the words like a cat on a mouse. 'You never mentioned a car before.'

'D—didn't I?'

Dear God, it was becoming impossible to remember what she had and hadn't said! Why didn't she just give up this whole black farce now and admit the truth?

But then she saw Nathan's face and recalled how he had snatched up her words as if he suspected that she might not have been strictly honest. If he *knew* she had been lying, how might he react? Her heart quailed at the prospect and she knew she couldn't risk finding out.

'You never mentioned a car at all last night,' Nathan pursued the point inexorably. 'Why not?'

'I—didn't think.'

'Nathan——' George put in quietly, but his friend ignored his interjection.

'Where is this car now?'

'I—don't know.' That at least was true, though to Rowan's hypersensitive mind her declaration sounded weak and unconvincing. 'I ran out of petrol somewhere on the moors. I was walking for hours before I found this house. I'm sorry if I didn't mention it before—it just went out of my head.'

'And what else "went out of your head"?'

What had happened to the gentle, sympathetic Nathan she knew—or rather, thought she knew? What had caused that other man, the one she had glimpsed briefly before, to come out into the open so that now she saw him fully for the first time? Saw him—and feared him, Rowan admitted to herself, seeing the firm, determined set of Nathan's jaw that drew his mouth into a hard line, the coldness that made his eyes as hard as stone. George had described his friend as 'straight as they come', and clearly he was a man who detested any form of dishonesty—which made her heart lurch painfully at the thought of how he would react to discovering what had really happened.

'What else haven't you told us? What other important facts have you carefully neglected to mention?'

'I——'

'Nathan!'

Rowan's feeble attempt to speak and George's sharply warning use of his friend's name came simultaneously and, finding herself incapable of continuing, Rowan weakly left it to the doctor to speak again.

'I can't have Rowan upset like this, Nathan. It won't do her any good at all. Can't you see you're just frightening her? She'll forget anything she might know if you keep badgering her in this way.'

Apprehensively, Rowan saw the way Nathan stood tensely, a muscle at the corner of his mouth twitching under the strain of the way his mouth was clamped tightly shut, and she felt her own nerves tighten in expectation of the explosion she felt sure was about to come.

'I'm sorry.'

The apology was so unexpected that for a second or two it didn't register on Rowan's confused mind. But the initial wave of relief was destroyed by the realisation of how curt and *un*apologetic he had sounded, his tone telling her only too clearly that he wasn't genuinely convinced.

'You'll have to excuse me, I have things to do.' Nathan paused in the doorway, turning a dark-eyed gaze on Rowan's strained face, his expression impossible to read. 'I'll make arrangements to do something about your car—see if we can find it.'

'Not the police!' Rowan's private fears made the words impossible to bite back.

For a long, nerve-stretching minute Nathan considered the matter, giving Rowan unwanted time in which to recognise the foolishness of her outburst, the panic it had revealed—a panic she knew that Nathan was only too well aware of.

'Not the police,' he said at last, adding with ominous emphasis, 'At least, not just yet.'

CHAPTER FOUR

EVEN though it was late afternoon the sun still shone gloriously, beating down on Rowan as she lay on a lounger in the large, beautifully cared-for garden of Nathan's house, but she felt none of the relaxation that might have been expected to result from such a comfortable situation. Nathan had provided a selection of books and magazines—his sister was an inveterate reader of the latter, he had told her—but they lay unopened on the grass beside her. She was incapable of concentrating on anything other than the terrible situation she was in.

Rowan sighed and slumped despondently against the pastel cushion of the lounger, her fingers moving restlessly, pleating over and over again the bright cotton of the flowered skirt she wore, which she had borrowed from Alexa Kennedy's wardrobe. When George had left after pronouncing her fit to get up, Nathan had taken her to another bedroom just down the landing from the one in which she had slept, and had flung open a large double wardrobe.

'Take your pick,' he had said. 'There should be something here to suit you. And don't worry about what Alexa will think,' he added, seeing her dubious expression. 'My sister's a clothesaholic; she has more outfits than she has time to wear. I doubt if she'll even notice that you've borrowed something.'

How could she tell him that it wasn't the thought of borrowing the clothes but Nathan's own attitude that was troubling her? When he had returned to the bedroom at George's summons she had sensed at once that the warm, sensitive man she had been so attracted to had been replaced by another person, one who was rigidly in control of himself, whose every word was

spoken in a coolly distant tone, but always with a hint
of some other emotion, one that was ruthlessly suppressed, making her feel as if she were stranded in the
middle of a minefield where some unwary move would
cause a devastating explosion right in her face.

He had organised a search for her car and would let
her know as soon as anything developed, he had told
her, his tone carefully neutral. But Rowan couldn't
forget the way he had rounded on her earlier, the
accusations of keeping things back he had flung at her.
Her outburst about the police had aroused his suspicions, she knew, and it was only George's strict
instructions that she was not to be upset that kept him
from launching into another attack, something she
feared even more than before because she felt so
desperately vulnerable to his attitude towards her.

Because the truth was that, even though Nathan
now appeared to be a very different man from the one
who had cared for her when she had first woken, she
still felt that overwhelming attraction towards him. All
through the uncomfortably silent lunch, which they
had eaten on a terrace leading into the garden, she had
been unable to stop her eyes from straying over the
firm, clean lines of his face, the lithe strength of his
body, finding herself hypersensitive to the movements
of his long, square-tipped fingers, the dark pools of his
eyes and the glossy sheen of his dark hair in the bright
sunlight.

She longed to be able to talk to him properly, hear
his deep voice tell her about himself, his life, his
family. She wanted to know what interested him, what
he did in such free time as the demands of his business
left him, but the wall of lies she had built round herself
was firm and solid, with no doorway nor even a tiny
crack through which she could try to reach him, and
Nathan himself seemed withdrawn and absorbed in his
own thoughts, so that what conversation they had was
stilted and awkward.

George had warned her that it might be like that.

'Don't let Nathan worry you,' he had said when Nathan had left the bedroom in order to organise the search for the car. 'He's not himself at the moment. Yesterday was——' he paused, seeming to have to hunt for a suitable phrase '—a difficult time for him for lots of reasons—none of them to do with you. He needs time to think things through, then he'll be OK. Just remember he's got things on his mind.'

'Business worries?'

'No—more personal matters. Nothing for you to worry about—you've enough to concern you with your own problems.'

If only George knew just how right he was, Rowan reflected miserably. But all the same it was impossible not to wonder just what 'personal matters' absorbed Nathan, the thought that she was only adding to his problems by being here making her want to crawl into a hole and hide.

If she had thought she could get away with it she would have left the house and fled, heading down the road to heaven knew where, but since he had installed her in the garden Nathan, probably on George's instructions, had scrupulously checked on her every half-hour or so—though in the intervening time he left her strictly alone. And, on a more practical note, she had nothing to put on her feet. Nathan had returned her handbag to her but, possibly suspecting she might try some sort of escape attempt, he had kept her shoes, and all the footwear in Alexa's wardrobe had been far too large.

Ruefully Rowan surveyed the black skirt patterned with red and blue flowers that she wore with a red cotton T-shirt. The skirt was rather too long—clearly Alexa Kennedy shared something of her brother's height—but it fitted well enough. She knew from Nathan's expression when she had finally made her way downstairs that she had surprised him by choosing such a simple outfit from the array of clothes in his sister's wardrobe. Recalling his comment about the white dress she had worn on the previous day, she had felt a bitter taste in her mouth as she had reflected that he couldn't know that she had deliberately chosen the least expensive items she could find because all her former pleasure in well-styled, costly clothes was now tainted by the shadow of her own secret guilt.

'Everything OK?'

There was nothing even remotely threatening about the quietly spoken words that interrupted her thoughts, but nevertheless they had Rowan starting nervously, sitting upright hastily, her eyes, wide and very blue, swinging to Nathan's face.

'Fine,' she managed, her voice shaking in a way that revealed her unease far too clearly for comfort as she struggled to push her unpleasant memories to the back of her mind, in order to be able to face him with some degree of confidence.

'No headache—dizziness?'

'None—honest.' She added the second word hastily when the swift narrowing of his eyes revealed that he had noticed the way she had lost colour as a result of the shock of his appearance. 'I'm feeling a lot better.'

They had had this conversation, the details perhaps varying slightly each time, at frequent intervals during the afternoon. Nathan would appear, ask how she was feeling—she could almost see him ticking off in his mind the points George had warned him to keep an eye out for—and then he would go away again, back to whatever private matters absorbed him inside the house.

Each time Rowan had longed to ask him to stay— once she had even opened her mouth to form the words, but had then hastily closed it again, knowing that if he did stay she would not be able to find anything to say to him. Her exile in the garden was like an unspoken but very pointed message, driving home to her more eloquently than words could ever do the fact that she was excluded from the personal side of Nathan's life, and she didn't feel that he would welcome her company even if she offered it.

But this time she didn't think she could bear to be left alone any longer. If, following his usual pattern, Nathan turned on his heel the moment his check had been completed and strode back into the house, she felt she would be unable to control her distress, would cry out, catch hold of his arm, plead for him to stay, if only for a moment.

But to her surprise Nathan showed no sign of leaving. Instead he hooked one of the garden chairs towards him with his foot and lowered himself into it. Only then did Rowan notice that in one hand he held a pair of delicate fluted glasses while a green glass bottle hung from the other.

'I thought you might be thirsty, so——' he lifted the bottle slightly '—I've brought some refreshment.'

Totally bemused by his sudden change in attitude, Rowan stared at the label on the bottle, her mouth slightly open in surprise.

'Champagne!'

Her voice was sharp with incredulity mixed with unease, as in the back of her mind she could hear Nathan's voice, touched with dark cynicism, saying to George, 'There's plenty of champagne. I reckon I'll be drinking the stuff for months.' In response, George had laid a hand on his friend's arm, she recalled, in a gesture of complete understanding, revealing his sympathy without a word having to be said. But Rowan had no idea what was behind Nathan's sardonic remark, and so now she felt completely out of her depth, that feeling growing worse as she heard Nathan speak ironically.

'The very best.' He was concentrating on pouring the wine into the glasses as if his life depended on not spilling a single drop. 'Perfect for any sort of celebration.' The satirical note in his voice had deepened, becoming a bitter emphasis, one that made Rowan's hand unsteady as she took the glass he held out to her.

'*Are* we celebrating?'

The glance he slanted at her through thick, dark lashes was filled with a mocking humour. 'That depends on how you look at it,' he returned obscurely.

'Look at what?' Rowan's voice was distinctly uneven. She couldn't understand this new, grimly humorous mood, and she didn't know how to cope with it.

'Life, I suppose.' Nathan took a long swallow of his drink, then held his glass up towards the sun, studying the bubbles sparkling in its light. 'They've found the car.'

It came so offhandedly, almost thrown away, that, in her confusion, Rowan barely registered what he had said.

'Found the——?'

When his dark eyes swung to her, keen and searching, she felt a shiver run down her spine in spite of the heat of the sun.

'They've found *your* car,' he amended pointedly.

'Oh, that's great!' If she had really lost her memory, then surely this information would delight her—wouldn't it? 'Where was it?'

'On the Summerbridge road; about seven miles from here. You walked a long way.'

'Yes, I did.' Seven miles? It had seemed like seventy at the time. The memory of her state of mind as she had tramped along the deserted road had Rowan taking a hasty sip of her champagne, and immediately wishing she hadn't as she saw Nathan's eyes flick downwards to follow the small, betraying movement. 'Where is it now? My car, I mean.'

If the truth were told, she didn't give a damn about her car. Like her clothes, it was just another reminder of her guilt, another weight around her neck, but Nathan would expect her to want to know, and not to ask would instantly arouse his suspicions.

'Was there anything inside it that might help?'

'I've made arrangements to have it towed here. As to what's inside it, I couldn't say. It was locked.'

Of course. Even in her confusion and despair, Rowan remembered that she had paused to lock her car before starting on the long walk to find help. Thinking back, she was amazed that she had actually had the presence of mind to do anything so practical.

'I must have done that automatically.'

One dark eyebrow lifted a fraction as Nathan absorbed that comment, and Rowan tensed, wondering if her unwary words would spark off another spate of questions, perhaps even another accusation of holding things back. But she was forgetting George's final instructions before he left.

'I want Rowan kept completely quiet, Nathan,' he had said firmly. 'She mustn't be disturbed in any way.' And throughout the rest of the day Nathan had stuck strictly to his role of nurse, never once coming close to the dangerous, aggressive mood he had displayed earlier that morning.

'Is that what we're celebrating—the fact that my car's been found?' she asked unevenly when the silence between them began to prey on her nerves.

'Mmm.'

Nathan's murmur might or might not have been one of agreement. His eyes had drifted away from her and he was staring out across the huge lawn, a thoughtful frown on his face.

Rowan recalled how, earlier, too restless to sit still, she had strolled around this part of the garden which, being at the back of the house, was completely hidden from the road. Around the edges, the lawn's smooth green surface had been pitted with holes, all evenly spaced, as if fairly recently someone had erected a large tent which had now been taken down. At the time she had thought nothing of it, but now, recalling Nathan's comment about the fact that he had been going to be married, a bitter twist to his mouth, she was forced to connect the two apparently disparate facts and wonder if the tent could have been the sort of marquee used for wedding receptions, and whether Nathan's cancelled wedding could have been more recent than she had believed, perhaps even in the last couple of months.

Her eyes went back to Nathan's absorbed face and she couldn't help wondering what he was thinking behind those hooded, dark eyes. Personal matters, George had said, so could those personal matters be his ruined marriage plans? She didn't dare ask, but a sudden rush of longing to know more about this man overwhelmed any thought of caution as she rushed into hasty speech.

'Tell me about your sister. Is she older or younger than you?'

'Alexa?' Nathan spoke vaguely, seeming to have to make an effort to drag his thoughts away from the subject that had occupied them. 'She's twenty-five—five years younger than me.'

It was like speaking to a robot, Rowan reflected wryly. He had answered her question, but automatically, speaking abstractedly without any real involvement in what he was saying.

'What does she do?'

'She's personnel manager for the firm.'

No elaboration, Rowan noted; no explanation as to what 'the firm' was, which implied that he was well aware that she already knew about Kennedy Construction. George must have told him that she had been asking questions.

'And she's on holiday at the moment?'

To her surprise, Nathan shook his dark head.

'Not on holiday. She's at work today, but she's staying with some friends in town for the week. Like I said, I wanted some time on my own.'

Quietly, unemphatically spoken though they were, his words still stung like the flick of a whip, stunning Rowan with the sudden sharp pain they inflicted. 'I'm sorry. I——'

'No,' Nathan lifted a hand in a gesture that erased his earlier words, '*I'm* sorry. I didn't mean that the way it sounded. Look, we've been over this already. You couldn't help what happened to you—you had an accident and you needed help. In a way, I'm glad you're here; it takes my mind off. . .'

He let the sentence trail off as he swallowed the last of the champagne in his glass, and in her mind Rowan tried to finish it for him. 'It takes my mind off. . .' what? Just what were those 'personal matters' that troubled him? Not Alexa, evidently—there had been no trace of concern in his voice when he'd spoken of his sister. But clearly that was an area into which he was not prepared to go, so she stuck to a safer path instead.

'Have you any other family? Your parents?'

'My father died seven years ago. My mother married again and now she lives in London with her second husband. There's another sister—Lesley. She comes between Alexa and me in age. She's married to Martin, who owns a farm on the other side of the valley.'

Nathan answered her questions easily enough—no one could have accused him of being unduly reticent—but his flat, lifeless monotone revealed that his heart wasn't in his answers, his attention still directed elsewhere. And that was something for which Rowan was deeply grateful, because the revelation that Nathan's father was dead and that his mother had remarried had affected her strongly. Here was something that they had in common, something she would have liked to share with him, to talk about on a much deeper level than the superficial, casual conversation she was obliged to pursue. But the lies she had told, the fact that she wasn't supposed to remember her parents and her own family situation, must always come between them.

'More champagne?' Nathan lifted the bottle from the lawn at his side.

'I—— Oh, why not?'

Perhaps the alcohol would relax her. Right now, she felt as if the lounger on which she sat were stuffed with prickly gorse and thistles, keeping her tense and on edge all the time. But she must be careful not to get *too* relaxed. If she did she might let slip something that was dangerously revealing.

The champagne that Nathan had drunk didn't seem to have affected him at all, she reflected, as he filled her glass with a sober concentration that made a mockery of the sparkling wine's connotations of gaiety and enjoyment. If it had been his intention to celebrate the discovery of her car, then his expression certainly didn't fit with that mood. His sombre seriousness would have gone down better at a wake.

'You've got quite a family, then,' she said, in an effort to stop the conversation from dying on its feet as Nathan subsided into silence once more. A pang of envy twisted in her heart at the thought that perhaps if she had had a brother or a sister herself she might have been able to talk things over with them, ask their advice, their help, and then she might never have found herself in the predicament that now blighted her life and out of which she could see no possible way of escape.

'Are you close to each other?'

'Close enough. I think we all know that if we need anyone the family's there—but equally we know that sometimes it's better to keep our distance and let the other person sort things out for themselves.'

Like now, Rowan thought. Now, when Nathan, by his own admission, had wanted to be left alone. Her conscience stung unmercifully at the way she had intruded into the peace and quiet he sought. Nathan had said it didn't matter, but then he didn't know the truth, had no idea how terribly she had deceived him. She did, and as a result doubted if she'd ever be able to live at ease with herself again.

Her eyes went back to Nathan, wandering over the strongly carved face that was turned towards the sun, his eyes half closed. If she had been able to turn to *him* before things had got too bad, he would have helped her, she was sure of that. He wouldn't have been soft with her—she doubted if he had a cell in his body that could be termed indulgent—but he would have got her back on the right track before it was too late. But now it was too late, far, far too late even to tell him the truth. The wall of lies was as solid as rock, an impregnable barrier to any real communication.

Surreptitiously Rowan studied the forceful structure of Nathan's face, her gaze lingering on the unexpected softness of his mouth, and she shifted uneasily in her seat, swallowing a rash amount of champagne as she found herself in the grip of an irrational longing to know the feel of those lips on hers. Her imagination running out of control, she thought of them sliding over her skin, along the delicate length of her throat, and down——

With a jolting shock she became aware that Nathan had spoken but, lost in her impossible dream, she hadn't heard a word he'd said.

'I'm sorry—what did you say?'

Did the huskiness of her voice reveal the sensual path down which her thoughts had been heading? Rowan felt burning hot and then shiveringly cold at the thought that Nathan might be able to guess what had been in her mind.

'I said, what about your family, Rowan? Can you tell me anything about them?'

Nervously Rowan brushed a hand across her face to break the contact of the searching gaze that seemed to burn her skin where it rested. 'I—— No, I can't. I've tried all day and. . .' Her head swam as she looked into those deep, dark eyes that seemed to have the power to draw her out of herself, so that her mind seemed to split in two as the longing to tell him everything warred with the need to maintain the fantasy she had created. A feeling of faintness swept over her and she had to grip the arms of the lounger, afraid that she might actualy fall.

'I can't remember, Nathan!' Unnervingly, that was now actually true. She couldn't picture her mother's face, or Bernard's. Even Colin's seemed to have been wiped from her mind. It seemed as if her life beyond this house, this man, had never existed, and that fact put a new intensity into her voice when she spoke again. 'I know you think I'm lying——'

But that was too much; the words caught in her throat, choking her.

'Not lying, Rowan,' Nathan put in quietly. 'I don't think you know what you're doing.'

'But this morning—you attacked me!'

'No, Rowan. I *challenged* you. You let slip something you hadn't told me before and I had to be sure that there wasn't anything else. I want to help you, but you have to let me. You have to help yourself.'

Those deep grey eyes locked with Rowan's wide blue ones, holding her mesmerised. She felt as if she were being drawn into a dark, fathomless pool, and every instinct told her that after this moment her life would never be the same again.

Tell him! her conscience screamed at her. Tell him now, while his mind is open to you. Drowning in the intensity of his gaze, she knew a tiny flare of hope that perhaps, if she did tell him, Nathan would listen, would help her as he had said he wanted to. Nervously she wetted her painfully dry lips with her tongue, but before she could say anything Nathan spoke again.

'Let me ring your family, Rowan. They must be frantic with worry about what's happened to you. Let me at least contact them and tell them you're safe.'

That was the last thing she wanted—and yet the thing she wanted most. Her mother would be desperately worried about her disappearance, and she hated the thought of being the cause of such anxiety. But if her mother knew where to find her then, inevitably, so would Bernard—and Colin.

'Not yet,' she whispered weakly.

'What are you running away from, Rowan?' Nathan's voice had sharpened noticeably. 'What are you so afraid of?'

Panic flared in Rowan's mind, driving away the dictates of her conscience. 'I'm not running from anything!' With a terrible feeling of despair she knew that yet another brick had been pushed into the wall of lies. 'I just can't remember—can't you accept that? I'm not afraid of anything. I've forgotten—it's lost!'

'But that's just the point. You haven't lost it. It's all still there, but your mind won't let you recall it. You can't solve your problems by running from them, Rowan. The only way to face them is to tackle them squarely. If you just let the barriers down——'

'*No*! Nathan, please!'

Suddenly she saw his face change, the intent, challenging light fading from his eyes as he took in her ashen face, her over-bright eyes, and he pushed a rough hand through his hair.

'Oh, hell, I'm going about this the wrong way. George warned me to take things slowly, but I'm too damn impatient.'

Rowan wanted to curl into a tight ball of misery. She could well imagine exactly why he felt so impatient. In spite of all his protestations, his assurances that her presence here didn't matter, he still wanted that time to himself. He wanted her to find out who she was and where she belonged so that she could be on her way out of his house—and out of his life.

'I'm sorry, Rowan.' Once more that long hand raked through his hair. 'I seem to be saying that a lot—but I *am* sorry. I didn't mean to upset you. It's just——'

'You've got other things on your mind,' Rowan put in dully.

'Yeah.' Nathan's self-deprecatory grin was wry, lopsided and boyishly attractive in a way that made Rowan's heart twist deep inside her. 'Poor Rowan.'

The sudden softness of his tone was somehow shocking after his challenging insistence, stunning her into immobility as he leaned forward to cup her cheek in his hand, his palm warm against her skin. Immediately Rowan felt her whole body quiver into life, as if that casual touch had flicked a switch that sent a current of electricity running through her. The temptation to turn her face into his hand, press a kiss against his fingers, was almost irresistible, but an instinctive awareness of the fact that that would be the wrong move to make combined with her guilty conscience to hold her still.

'You come here, lost and alone, looking for help, and all you find is a man who's got problems of his own—whose mind's on other things.'

Rowan's throat was painfully dry, so it was an effort to speak, but she had to ask; she had to know. 'What sort of problems, Nathan? George said personal matters—I don't want you to think that I'm prying, but. . .'

Her voice trailed off as Nathan shook his head. 'Don't bother yourself about it, Rowan. You've enough on your plate as it is. They're my problems—I'll work them out.'

'But if I could help in any way——'

'Rowan, leave it!' Nathan took his hand away abruptly and reached for the bottle of champagne. 'Let's have another drink.'

'Drowning your sorrows?' Rowan couldn't suppress the satirical note in her voice. Nathan's rejection of her offer to help had piqued her more than she cared to admit—even to herself.

'Damn you, Rowan, I said leave it!'

The sudden silence that followed Nathan's angry explosion was broken by the sound of the telephone ringing inside the house, and immediately Rowan's mind went back to the moment when she had first arrived at the house on the previous day. The telephone had been ringing then; it was the last thing she had registered before she had fainted—and Nathan had been dressed so very differently, sleek and elegant in that superbly tailored suit, his tie hanging loose round his neck.

'Yesterday—when I arrived—you were on your way out.'

Nathan had got to his feet to answer the summons of the telephone, but now he paused, turning back to her, his eyes almost black in the closed, shuttered mask that his face had become. Everything about his stance, the tautly held muscles of his body, warned her that she had come too close, that if she had any sense she would stop now, before she got on to dangerous ground.

But Rowan couldn't stop, though his tension communicated itself to her, tightening her throat so that her voice was husky and uneven as she forced her words past the knot that seemed to have formed in it. 'You were dressed for something special—but because of me you never got there. Nathan, I *have* to know— were you going somewhere important?'

For a long, nerve-tightening minute she thought he wasn't going to answer her, and the persistent sound of the telephone bell shrilled imperiously in the taut silence. Then Nathan's mouth twisted in the cynical way she had seen before.

'I suppose you could say that,' he drawled in a darkly sardonic tone. 'I did have something "special" planned for yesterday—I was supposed to be getting married.'

CHAPTER FIVE

GEORGE had left a bottle of mild sedatives to help Rowan sleep if she needed them, but, wanting to keep a clear head in order to do some serious thinking, she had adamantly refused to take any—a decision she was now beginning to regret as the dark minutes of the night lengthened into hours, leaving her more desolate than before and incapable of finding any answer to her problems except one.

She had to tell Nathan the truth; tell him and go— get out of his life and leave him in peace. She had thought she was incapable of feeling any worse about the situation in which she had entangled herself, but Nathan's declaration that yesterday should have been his wedding day had left her feeling like the lowest form of life imaginable.

How could she stay here now? Nathan hadn't elaborated on his stark statement. He had simply flung it in her face and stalked away to answer the summons of the telephone, leaving Rowan with a thousand disturbed thoughts whirling inside her head.

What *had* happened after she had fainted? Had Nathan telephoned the church or register office explaining that, due to circumstances beyond his control—because of *her*—he couldn't get to the wedding? Dear God, what had his family, his friends—his *bride*—thought of that? Clearly, the girl he had been going to marry—what was her name? Meryl?—had reacted badly. Nathan's cynicism when he had referred to his ruined plans made it plain that she had not accepted his explanation—and who could blame her? How could any woman accept that the man she was going to marry had called off the ceremony because some total stranger had blundered into his life?

70

Rowan tossed and turned restlessly in her bed. The room was stifling, the warm sunlight of the day having changed to the close atmosphere and oppressive heat that usually preceded a thunderstorm, and she flung the bedclothes away from her in an attempt to cool her overheated body.

She had felt so close to Nathan, had known intuitively that he had the potential to be a very special person in her life. A raging heat that had nothing to do with the weather suffused her body. She had felt desire, passion towards him in a way that she had never experienced in her life before—and he had been going to marry someone else.

Phrases heard but not understood during the past two days pounded in her head, tormenting her because now she knew what they really meant.

'I never expected to be here tonight. I thought I'd be miles away.' On his *honeymoon*!

'George was going to be my best——'

And finally, the most disturbing of all, 'I'm not married. I was going to be, but—things changed.'

Bitterly, Rowan recalled how Nathan had spoken to George, his voice low-toned, not wanting her to hear.

'It's been one hell of a day, what with Meryl—and now this.'

This meant her; her unwanted presence in his house, the unwitting cause of those 'personal matters' he had on his mind. She had seen Nathan's home as a refuge, a place of safety from her own troubles, but in fact by being here she had increased those problems one hundredfold.

All this was the result of her own cowardice, her refusal to face up to what she had done. Nathan had been right: running away solved nothing. The only way to deal with the situation was to face it squarely and take the consequences. Only then could she ever hope to be free of the guilt and anxiety that came in the wake of her foolish actions.

She had to tell Nathan the truth. She could never

live with herself if she didn't. And, although her heart
quailed inside her at the prospect, although she knew
that there could be only one possible result—that
Nathan would immediately turn from her in revulsion
and disgust—she knew, as exhaustion finally claimed
her, that it was the only thing she could do.

The church was packed. On either side, smiling faces
turned to her as, dressed in a breathtakingly beautiful
white gown, she moved slowly down the aisle. She saw
her mother, resplendent in a spectacular outfit and
huge hat, turn towards her, her eyes filling with joyful
tears, but allowed herself only a moment to smile back,
her whole attention concentrated on the altar steps
where Nathan waited for her.

It *was* Nathan. Even though his back was towards
her and she couldn't see his face, she knew it could be
no one else. No other man stood tall and proud like
that, his dark head gleaming in a shaft of sunlight that
filtered through a nearby window. And, besides, she
recognised the grey pin-striped suit that he had been
wearing when he'd first opened the door to her—his
wedding suit.

In a haze of happiness she listened to the traditional
words of the wedding service.

'Do you, Meryl, take this man. . .?'

It was a pity about the mistake with her name, but
she wasn't going to let that worry her. Nothing could
spoil this, the most wonderful, magical, glorious day of
her life. She wasn't aware of Nathan saying, 'I do,'
which was strange, because those were the words she
most longed to hear—the only words that mattered—
but she heard her own voice saying them loud and
clear, not a trace of hesitancy or uncertainty in her
confident tone.

'I now pronounce you man and wife. You may kiss
the bride.'

Rowan turned her face towards Nathan as strong
hands slowly lifted the veil that covered her face. Her

heart was beating in strong, rapid strokes, her breathing quickening, her lips parting in a smile, ready to receive this, her first kiss as Nathan's wife.

But then the world reeled round her as she stared not at Nathan, but into the gloating, triumphant face of—*Colin!*

'*No!*'

In panic she tried to swing away, wanting only to run, to flee from him, but cruel hands held her back, dragging her inexorably closer, closer, until she could feel his breath against her cheek.

'A favour for a favour, Rowan,' he sneered, his words burning into her like acid. '*Anything*, you said— anything I asked—and now I'm asking. I've always wanted you, Rowan, ever since I first saw you, and now I've got you. Now you're mine—mine—mine.'

'No! No! Oh, please—*no!*'

'Rowan? *Rowan!*'

At first Rowan thought that the voice she heard and the arms that held her were still part of her dream, and she struggled frantically, lashing out with her fists in panic, only jolting into wakefulness with the realisation that her blows were landing on solid, warm flesh.

'Rowan, wake up!'

Not Colin's voice, she registered vaguely—but a voice she knew; a voice that promised help and safety if she could only——

'Rowan, you have to wake up! It's only a dream—a nightmare. If you open your eyes it will all go away.'

'*Open your eyes.*' She didn't want to open her eyes, terrified that if she did she would see Colin's face, his brown eyes bright with malevolent joy. But she trusted that voice, believed in it, would do anything it asked.

With a groan she forced her heavy eyelids open and, as in those brief moments of waking the day before, found herself looking straight into a pair of watchful, deeply concerned dark grey eyes.

'Nathan!'

It was a sigh of pure release; the relief so great that

she sagged against him weakly, her cheek resting against his chest. The solid, steady beat of his heart eased the frantic racing of her own pulse as she drew a long, sobbing breath.

'Oh, Nathan, it was——'

'It was just a dream,' Nathan put in firmly. 'You were dreaming, Rowan. None of it was real.'

But some of it was, Rowan thought unhappily. Colin's threatening triumph had been only too real, and the words he had spoken hadn't been created by her imagination, but were the ones she had heard him speak only days before. And the priest had said 'Meryl', the name of Nathan's fiancée. It had been Nathan's wedding she had been dreaming of, the marriage she had ruined unwittingly—but all her own black memories had combined to create the nightmare.

Strangely, one person had been missing. Why hadn't Roy been there? If her mind had been replaying the events in the past that had brought her to this situation, then surely Roy should have been there in the middle of it? After all, he had been the start of it all. But then, of course, she had never really cared for Roy. She had liked him, had enjoyed being with him, had trusted him in contrast to Colin, but that was all. A bitter laugh almost escaped her lips. She had *trusted* him. Oh, what a fool she'd been!

'Put it out of your mind, Rowan,' Nathan urged softly. 'It was only a dream—it doesn't matter.'

Numbly Rowan shook her head, an aching sense of longing uncoiling in the pit of her stomach as she felt the way her cheek brushed against the rough hairs on his chest, which was naked above the dark blue pyjama trousers he wore. Unable to bear his closeness when she had just admitted to the full extent of the chasm that lay between them, she jerked away from him, wrenching herself out of his arms with a violence that tore at her heart.

'It wasn't just a dream, Nathan. There were people. . .'

Her voice failed her as in her mind's eye she saw once again Colin's leering, triumphant face. *That* was real—a living nightmare she could never shake off, one that became so much worse when she was awake. Through a fog of misery she heard Nathan's muffled curse.

'I knew it! It's the car, isn't it? That's what brought this on.'

At first, confused and bewildered, Rowan couldn't understand what he meant, but then realisation dawned and she had to bite down hard on her lower lip to stop herself from groaning aloud.

Nathan had been a long time answering the telephone call that had taken him away from her after the devastating declaration he had made in the garden, and when he'd come back to Rowan he'd clearly had himself once more totally in control, his face closed against her so that she knew without a word being spoken that the subject of his marriage was forbidden territory, and any attempt to reopen it would be met with a blank wall of resistance.

'Your car's arrived,' he had announced stiffly. 'You'd better come and have a look at it, check that everything's all right.'

He had insisted that she went over every inch of the car with a concern for detail that had seemed to Rowan, her mind still in a state of shock after his revelation, to be totally unnecessary, getting into the vehicle himself to check the glove compartment, opening the boot, his actions reminding her strongly of those of a detective hunting for clues in all the crime films she had ever seen.

Belatedly she now realised that hunting for clues had been exactly what he *had* been doing. He had wanted her to check the car so thoroughly because he had thought that something in it might remind her of her 'forgotten' past. And now he thought that the nightmare that had gripped her had been sparked off by something she had seen and registered unconsciously which had risen to the surface of her mind while she was asleep.

'Look.' The gentleness of Nathan's tone was like a bitter reproach, stinging like acid on her guilt-sensitised nerves. 'You've had a shock—a fright. Why don't you come downstairs for a while? I'll make a drink and we can talk things through. Where's your robe?'

The question brought a wash of colour to Rowan's cheeks as she realised that all she was wearing was a nightdress which, once again, she had borrowed from the absent Alexa's wardrobe. Clearly Alexa Kennedy went for glamour rather than practicality, and the nightdress had only the merest suggestion of a bodice, with what there was held up by shoestring straps and plunging to a deep V over the soft curves of her breasts, revealing more than it concealed. Although, in a bikini, she had often worn far less than this, that had been on the beach, not in the intimate surroundings of a bedroom, and never with a man who made her so intensely aware of her own femininity as Nathan beside her.

Instinctively her hands reached for the sheet to cover herself, but then a flash of cold reason stilled the movement. What did it matter what Nathan saw? He had shown no interest in her sexually at all—and now she knew why. His love, his desire, were all given to Meryl, the woman he should have married.

And yet there had been that moment on the day she'd arrived when she had first woken and he had said that she shouldn't be ashamed of her body. The memory of the sensual smile that had accompanied his words suddenly made it imperative that she covered up at once.

'Over there.'

A jerky, awkward movement of her hand indicated where the pink and white robe lay across a chair on the other side of the room. When Nathan held it out to her she snatched it from him, shoving her arms into the sleeves with a haste and clumsiness that was the result of the way her body was shaking in reaction to that one brief memory, her reaction made all the more acute by the belated realisation of just how little Nathan himself was wearing—a fact which set her heart fluttering like a trapped butterfly.

Did she want to go downstairs? Could she bear to be alone with Nathan in the silence and darkness of the night, feeling as she did about him? Could she possibly 'talk things through' with him as he had suggested? But if she didn't go down and have that drink that Nathan had suggested she strongly suspected that he would stay with her, in the bedroom, and that was more than she could cope with.

'Why don't you go on down?' she managed shakily. 'I'll join you in a minute—I just want to freshen up a bit first. I feel terribly sweaty and sticky.'

In the bathroom she splashed cold water on her face and held her wrists under the running tap in an effort to calm her uneven pulse as she surveyed her reflection in the mirror. Her skin looked ashen, colourless in contrast to the blue-black sheen of her boyishly short hair, and above her pallid cheeks her blue eyes had a stunned, bruised look. There was an expression in them which made it hard for her to meet them directly, and she glanced away swiftly instead.

The impact of that tiny movement hit home like a blow to Rowan's stomach. 'What are you running away from?' In her mind she heard Nathan's voice as clearly as if he had actually been standing behind her, and all at once she knew with a desperate certainty that the time had come for the truth—and only the truth would do.

If she was ever going to be able to look herself or anyone else in the eye ever again, she *had* to stop running. She had to turn and face facts squarely—and take the consequences. With a determined movement Rowan tied the belt of her robe firmly round her waist and straightened her shoulders, lifting her chin high as she headed for the stairs.

'I've poured you a brandy.' Nathan indicated the glass on the coffee-table. 'I've made coffee too, but I thought you'd need something to help you over the shock of your nightmare.'

'Are you having one?'

He would need it, she reflected miserably. When she'd told him everything she had to say he would be the one in a state of shock, not her.

'Not for me, thanks. If I'm to help you I'd better keep a clear mind—and that champagne this afternoon went straight to my head.'

Had it? Rowan found that hard to believe. From the coolly distant way Nathan had behaved all evening she would have said that he wasn't even remotely intoxicated—or perhaps he meant that under the influence of alcohol he had admitted that he had been on his way to his wedding when she had arrived at the house, something he now clearly wished he had never revealed.

'I'll stick to coffee, anyway. Come and sit down.' He held out a hand to guide her to her seat and, still hypersensitive to the impact of his physical presence, Rowan flinched away from his touch. If he had put some more clothes on she might have felt better, but the night was uncomfortably warm and Nathan still wore only the pyjama trousers, his powerful torso, now seen in the light instead of the shadowy darkness of the bedroom, disturbingly tanned and tautly muscled.

'I'm sorry,' she murmured hastily, seeing Nathan's quick frown. 'It's just—I'm still——'

'Still upset? Don't worry, I'll not push you. Take your time, and when you're ready we'll talk.'

Nathan's ready sympathy and understanding were almost more than Rowan could bear. They had her reaching for the brandy glass with a haste that must have made her appear like some confirmed alcoholic, needing a fix as much as any junkie. After a couple of sips of the fiery spirit she felt a new warmth begin to creep through her veins, making her feel slightly less as if every muscle and nerve were being stretched tight on some medieval torture rack.

The sensation was only temporary though, her tension reviving with a new vengeance as Nathan, having poured two mugs of coffee, placed one in front of her and, with the other in his hand, installed himself in the armchair directly opposite her. He seemed prepared to wait in silence until she was ready to speak, and that fact dried Rowan's throat. Unable to launch straight into the confession that she knew she had to make, she glanced desperately around the room, searching for some other topic of conversation, a gasp of shock escaping her as her gaze fell on the large clock on the mantelpiece.

'Quarter to three? Is that really the time? Oh, Nathan, I'm sorry!'

A dismissive shrug lifted Nathan's broad shoulders. 'Don't worry. I wasn't asleep anyway. And Meryl always said that the early hours of the morning were the best time to talk.' His eyes drifted away from her to stare, unfocused, at some point on the opposite wall. 'She said it was amazing how people changed almost as soon as the clock struck midnight—how they stopped talking trivia and began to open up, reveal the truth about themselves. The after-twelve complex, she called it.'

That dangerous word 'truth' had Rowan taking another unwary gulp of brandy, almost emptying the glass. 'Meryl—is she your——?' Rowan broke off abruptly, unable to find the right word to describe the other woman.

'My fiancée? Correction——' satire laced Nathan's tone '——ex-fiancée. Yes, that's Meryl.'

Rowan barely heard the final sentence, that appalling 'ex' reverberating in her head over and over again like the thud of heavy hammers against her skull. Just what had happened between Nathan and Meryl while she had been unconscious? Had Nathan telephoned his fiancée to explain that he was unavoidably detained, and had she said that if he didn't come now it was all over between them—finished? Her conscience stabbed at her agonisingly at the thought of how she had ruined Nathan's life. He had had his future all mapped out—marriage to the woman he loved, a family—and her arrival had snatched that future from him.

But what sort of woman was the unknown Meryl? If she had truly loved Nathan, wouldn't she have under-stood that he could hardly leave an apparently ill, distraught and desperate stranger to fend for herself even if it was his wedding day?

To her complete consternation, Rowan found that the torment of her conscience was mixed with a sudden rush of something worryingly close to delight at the thought that perhaps Nathan's fiancée hadn't really loved him. But then a swift rush of icy reality destroyed that tiny flare of hope. If Nathan had asked Meryl to marry him, then surely *he* had been deeply in love with her? The need to know more overcame all thought of tact or the wisdom of questioning him further.

'What's she like?'

'Meryl?' As it had been in the garden earlier, Nathan's tone was abstracted and somehow automatic. 'She's tall, blonde—*very* beautiful—and very talented. Her father's a major landowner in the area and Meryl runs her own interior design company.' A small, slightly lop-sided smile crossed Nathan's face and his tone had warmed perceptibly as he continued. 'She's an extremely intelligent, warm-hearted and very classy lady.'

And one eminently suited to becoming Mrs Nathan Kennedy, Rowan thought on a wave of anguish. The wealthy, independent, aristocratic Meryl would be a much more suitable wife for a man in Nathan's position than a penniless working girl with a murky past——

Suddenly conscious of the way her thoughts were heading, she pulled herself up sharply and downed the rest of her brandy, setting the glass down with a distinct crash that drew Nathan's eyes to her immediately.

'Do you want another?'

'No.'

She could do with another drink, Rowan reflected. After its initial impact, the brandy had had little effect on the frayed state of her nerves. But to sit here downing spirits by the glassful would give completely the wrong impression. Not that there was a *right* impression to give, stern reason forced her to admit. Nathan, the man George had described as 'straight as they come', would find nothing with which to sympathise in her tawdry little story.

'No, thanks,' she amended her gruff refusal hastily. 'I'll stick to coffee.'

'OK.' Nathan retrieved his own mug from the coffee-table. 'Are you ready to talk yet?'

She would never be ready. There was no way she could just launch into the tale she knew would drive Nathan away from her as effectively as if the earth had moved to open a great chasm between them. And what made matters worse was the fact that she desperately wanted to talk—but not about herself.

She wanted to hear all about Nathan; about his life and family, his interests, and most of all about Meryl. That warm note that had slid into Nathan's voice when he'd spoken of his ex-fiancée had told Rowan that the other woman was very special to him—but how deep did those feelings go?

One thing was certain: clearly Nathan had no intention of letting the conversation centre on him any more than it already had. The abstracted mood seemed to have left him, and that brisk, 'Are you ready to talk yet?' left her in no doubt that his concerns and feelings were forbidden territory, an area into which she strayed at her peril.

'What—what do you want to know?'

If he would only take control of the conversation,

ask questions, then perhaps she would find the courage
to get started.

'Perhaps we'd better begin with the dream. Can you
remember any of it?'

Rowan nodded silently. She could remember her
dream all right; she doubted if she would ever be able
to forget it. It seemed etched into her brain in images
of fire.

'Then what happened? What terrified you so much?'

She couldn't tell him about the dream wedding; *that*
had to remain buried in her mind forever.

'Colin——'

The name slipped out before she had time to think,
and she saw Nathan's head come up, his eyes narrowing swiftly.

'Colin?' he asked sharply. 'Who's he?'

'My stepbrother.'

She wasn't prepared for Nathan's smile, the sudden
rush of delight that curved his mouth into a wide,
unrestrained grin.

'Rowan, you remembered something! That's
fantastic!'

'No!'

She couldn't bear it, couldn't live with herself and
what she'd done. If she hadn't decided already, Rowan
knew that Nathan's reaction now would have convinced her once and for all that she couldn't continue
with this lie any longer. Her hand clenched around the
handle of her coffee-mug until her knuckles showed
white, and she drew in a long, uneven breath.

'Nathan—there's something I have to tell you.'

CHAPTER SIX

'GO ON,' Nathan prompted quietly, his words falling into the silence that had descended after Rowan had blurted out her declaration that she had something to tell him. Having said that, she found that her throat had closed up completely and she couldn't force another word past her stiff, dry lips. 'What is it you want to say?'

Then, as she struggled to form any response, he leaned forward in his seat, deep grey eyes probing her face, searching for his answer there.

'Have you remembered something else? Is that it?'

'Oh, Nathan!' Rowan found a voice at last, but, hoarse and unsteady, it didn't sound at all like her own. 'I've——'

Her mind flinched away from the words 'I've remembered', her conscience refusing to allow her to use them. If she was going to tell him anything, it had to be the complete truth and nothing less.

'I know *everything*—all about myself—everything that happened. I. . .' Even the shaky, uncertain voice failed her as she looked into Nathan's eyes and saw the deep, concerned sympathy that darkened them. How could she go on when what she had to say would wipe that expression from his face at a single stroke?

'Tell me!' The command came sharply. 'Rowan— *tell me!*' he went on when she still hesitated, the new and disturbing intensity of his tone making it sound for all the world as if knowing the truth about her were the most important thing in his life. 'Who *are* you?'

'Rowan Carey—but you know that. I'm twenty-two, and live in Carborough with my mother and stepfather, Bernard Stewart——'

'And Colin,' Nathan inserted, his tone surprisingly rough-edged.

'And Colin,' Rowan confirmed dully. She wasn't ready to talk about Colin yet. 'My father died when I was twelve and Mother met Bernard two years later. They were married on my fifteenth birthday.'

The image of Bernard's warm, open face, topped with a bush of curling salt-and-pepper hair slid into her mind and she closed her eyes against the pain and guilt the memory brought with it.

'You didn't get on with your stepfather?'

'No——' As she realised her mistake, her eyes flew open and unconsciously she leaned towards Nathan, her whole body expressing her need to tell the story properly.

'I mean yes. There wasn't any problem like that. Bernard's an angel, he adores my mother and he's always been wonderful to me.'

'Then it was Colin who was the problem.'

It had been a statement, not a question. Nathan was too perceptive for comfort. How had she ever thought she could hide anything from him?

'Yes, Colin was the problem.'

Colin and Roy—but if it hadn't been for Colin's tormenting behaviour she would probably never have turned to Roy in quite the same way. To her dismay Rowan felt bitter tears burn in her eyes, and she blinked furiously, determined not to let them fall. To resort to tears might make Nathan think she was playing on his sympathy, and that was not her intention at all.

Through a blurred haze she saw Nathan move, coming to sit close beside her, and she felt his hands, warm and strong, close on her own.

'Rowan, I know this is difficult for you, but you have to do it. You have to make yourself remember, because only then can you face up to whatever it is that's making you so unhappy. I know it's hard, but—— Oh, Rowan!'

Rowan knew why his tone had softened, and she cursed herself for it. Unable to control her emotions any more, she had given up the struggle and weakly let the tears cascade down her cheeks.

'Rowan!'

The next moment she was caught in a pair of powerful arms and drawn close against the warm strength of his chest, Nathan's instinctive gesture of comfort breaking down what was left of her self-control so that she gave a convulsive gasp and sobbed like a baby.

'Oh, *Rowan*!'

It was a low, husky murmur, and at first Rowan couldn't think what the brief warm sensation against her forehead might be. It was only when Nathan's mouth moved over her closed eyelids and down her cheek, his lips brushing away the tracks of her tears, that she realised what was happening, and by then she was beyond protesting or making any attempt to resist his kisses.

Acting on blind instinct, her mind too bruised and numb to do otherwise, she nestled closer to Nathan, her cheek sliding over the dampness where her tears had fallen on the skin of his chest, and lifted her face slightly, her heart jolting painfully as she felt his lips come down on hers.

It began as a gentle, tender kiss of comfort and sympathy, but Rowan needed more than that, the sweet excitement that the touch of his mouth on hers unleashed making her lips soften and open under his, her tongue emerging tentatively, enticing, encouraging, and she knew a heady thrill of delight as Nathan's arms tightened round her and he followed her lead without any sign of hesitation. The kiss deepened, becoming possessed of a passion that was almost savage in its intensity, his mouth crushing hers with a strength that sent a *frisson* of something close to fear shivering down her spine.

At last she had her desire. At last she was free to let

her hands wander over his body, over the warm, smooth skin, the firm muscles of his shoulders and chest, and up into the silky darkness of his hair, and she used that freedom joyfully, her caresses becoming more confident, more urgent as she found herself unable to hold back the feelings that had burned in her almost from the first moment she had seen him.

With a sudden twisting movement Nathan lifted her so that she was half lying across his knees, his hands tugging impatiently at the belt of her robe until it opened, the flimsy garment falling away to her sides. The delicate straps of the borrowed nightdress were no barrier to his searching fingers, and Rowan was unable to hold back the gasp of pure pleasure that escaped her as Nathan's hands closed over her breasts, cupping the soft flesh, his thumbs moving erotically over the hardened pink nipples.

'Rowan!'

Her name was a rough, thick sound in Nathan's throat and she vaguely heard her own voice sigh his name as a burning wave of desire suffused her body. She reached for him again, her hands linking round his neck to draw his face down to hers once more.

But Nathan's head stayed rigidly upright. With a cold sense of shock Rowan felt his stiff resistance and her eyes flew open, a sensation like the splash of icy water in her face freezing her into immobility as she looked at him, seeing the way his expression had changed, becoming hard as granite, even his eyes, which had burned with an inner fire only moments before, now as cold as tempered steel.

'This isn't right,' he said, his voice harsh and uneven. 'I never meant——'

At once the arms Rowan had linked around his neck loosened and fell to her sides as if she were a puppet whose strings had been cut. *Meryl*, she thought desolately, seeing Nathan lift a hand to cover his eyes and rub it violently against his forehead as if to erase the tormenting thoughts that plagued him. He's remembered Meryl.

Her aching, frustrated body screamed at her to override Nathan's scruples, to capture his head again, force aside that concealing hand and press her lips to his. She needed him, wanted him as she had never wanted any other man in her life, and the total despair that swamped her at the abrupt cessation of their lovemaking was like a savage pain in her heart.

But she could try every trick she knew, and some she hadn't learned until now—ones that her newly awakened body would teach her—and Nathan would never respond. Every instinct told her that as clearly as if the fragile barrier of his raised hand had been a steel door that had suddenly slammed shut between them. His kisses had only been meant to comfort her—*she* was the one who had taken them for something else because she had wanted it to be that way. Her actions, her response, had drawn him into something he had never intended.

Hadn't she learned anything from Roy? She knew only too well how a man could show passion and desire and yet not be emotionally involved in any way at all. In his loneliness, his distress at the loss of the girl he had been going to marry, Nathan had needed someone to hold, a warm, willing body to ease the emptiness inside—but that was all. She could have been anyone—who she was meant nothing. Meryl was the one who had Nathan's heart.

Her own heart just a devastated, rawly painful void, Rowan forced herself upright, moving slightly away from Nathan as her hands went automatically to pull the front of her nightdress up over her exposed and aching breasts, her mind flinching away from the recognition of the fact that the red patches that marked her creamy skin were the result of Nathan's urgent caresses. As she drew the sides of her robe together and fumbled for her belt Nathan stirred and sighed deeply.

'What can I say?' At last he removed the hand that had hidden his face and his dark eyes burned into her. 'Dear God, Rowan, I'm *sorry*. That should never have happened. It was terribly wrong of me. I. . .'

'*That should never have happened*.' Rowan brought her teeth down hard on her lower lip to keep back the cry of pain that rose in her throat. It should never have happened because to Nathan it meant nothing at all. It could have been anyone—*anyone*—she repeated the word, trying to drive it home.

But it hadn't been just anyone—it had been her—and her own reactions, the spiralling passion that even now made her body ache with unassuaged need, had taught her that the physical sensitivity she had felt towards Nathan from the start hadn't just been a temporary aberration brought about by shock and distress at the situation in which she found herself.

Roy had been a singularly attractive man, but he had never been able to light the fire that flared inside her at Nathan's slightest touch. No one else had ever made her forget herself so completely that she would have given herself to him right here on the settee—would still do so if that was what he asked. But Nathan would never ask, and that was what made her feel as if she were being slowly torn apart.

'Rowan, what can I say except that I'm desperately sorry?'

Rowan couldn't meet Nathan's eyes, couldn't bear to see in them the distress and shame she could hear so clearly in his voice, and she was terribly afraid that if she lifted her head he would read her own pain and longing in her face. So she kept her head bent, her hands toying nervously with the belt of the robe.

'It's all right.' Her voice was just a shaken whisper. 'Don't blame yourself. I understand.'

'You understand?' The rough edge of Nathan's uneven laughter made Rowan wince painfully. 'You *understand*?' he repeated with cynical emphasis. 'Hell and damnation, Rowan, I doubt if you do.'

Out of the corner of her eye Rowan saw how his hand lifted, moved towards her, hesitated and then was abruptly snatched away again to lie, clenched into a savage fist, against his side.

'I said I wanted to help, but instead I—— Oh, *God*, Rowan—I'm so damnably sorry!'

That final word, spoken in such tones of heartfelt self-reproach, tore at Rowan's heart, ripping away the shattered threads of such control as she had been able to impose on herself and leaving her raw and devastated and knowing only one thing—that she had to get everything out into the open *now*, if only to ease his mind. He wouldn't care what he had done when he knew the truth, wouldn't want her anywhere near him. He would want her gone, out of his life—and right now that was what she wanted, too. She couldn't bear to stay here any longer feeling as she did, and knowing that there was no way those feelings could be reciprocated. If Nathan sent her away it couldn't hurt her any more than the pain she was feeling now.

'You said you wanted to help,' she declared in a tight, brittle voice that rang sharply in the silence of the night. 'Well, there's only one way you *can* help—and that's by letting me tell you everything.'

'I'm listening,' Nathan said quietly.

The softness of his voice was almost more than Rowan could bear, and her hands tightened over the belt she still held as if she would tear it in two.

'Then don't say another word.'

If she heard his voice it would destroy her. She would remember its gentleness, the sympathy she had heard in it so often, and the words would shrivel in her throat.

'Just let me tell you—don't interrupt or ask questions. I promise I'll tell you everything.'

She sensed rather than saw the nod that, keeping strictly to her instructions to remain silent, was Nathan's only response, and, still keeping her head bent, she began in a flat, dull voice.

'As I said, my father died when I was twelve. He was a lot older than my mother, but all the same neither of us expected that it would happen quite so soon. I was devastated—we both were—and for a time Mother and I were completely lost. Eventually I began to pull round, but it seemed like the bottom had gone out of Mother's world; she just couldn't find any enthusiasm for anything. Then she met Bernard.'

Unknown to herself, Rowan's small, heart-shaped face softened as she spoke her stepfather's name. She owed Bernard such a lot—which was what made the way she had behaved so appalling.

'I knew he was right for her from the start. It was wonderful to see the way she came alive in his company, and I was overjoyed when they told me they'd decided to get married. Bernard helped and supported me, too. He encouraged me to go on a business course at college, and when I qualified he gave me a job with his firm—he owns a small building company in Boroughbridge.'

Rowan risked a tiny, surreptitious glance at Nathan's face and saw that what she had said had registered. She could almost hear his mind turning over, checking through facts, until a tiny nod indicated that, as she had expected, he had recalled the name Stewart Building and knew of the firm.

'At Christmas Bernard promoted me from being his secretary to handling the firm's books. I wasn't sure I could do it, but he had complete faith in me and I was delighted that I had his confidence and trust.' Rowan drew a long, shaky breath. 'The only fly in the ointment was Colin.'

A tiny movement from the man at her side startled her, making her realise that Nathan had been waiting for her to mention her stepbrother again. Abruptly she reached for her coffee-mug and cradled it in her hands, curling her fingers round it to try to draw some of its warmth into herself to counteract the coldness that was creeping over her in spite of the heavy warmth of the night, seeming to turn her blood to ice.

'Colin is two years older than me, and from the moment Mum and I moved into Bernard's house he made life very difficult for me. At first he was just thoroughly unpleasant, always making sarcastic comments, sneering at everything I enjoyed and generally putting me down, but later, when I came home from college, he changed and started to make it very clear that he—fancied me.'

Rowan's blue eyes became clouded and dull as she recalled her stepbrother's unwanted attentions.

'He was always pestering me, making excuses to touch me—the sort of thing that neither Bernard nor my mother would consider anything other than friendliness, but which I hated because I knew what was behind it. He'd asked me out a couple of times, but I'd refused. He's not at all like Bernard; he's slimy—he makes my skin creep. He believes that there's only one place for a woman—in his bed—and he was determined that I should be his next mistress. I tried everything I could to get my message across, but he wouldn't take no for an answer. He even started coming to my room when I was getting ready for bed— he'd just walk in without knocking.'

Rowan's voice became uneven as she recounted how, on one occasion, Colin had come into her room when she had just got out of the bath and was wearing only a towel wrapped around her. He had kicked the door shut, lounging back against it and subjecting her body to an insolently appraising scrutiny.

'You have a gorgeous body, little sister,' he had drawled. 'What a pity its promise isn't matched by that frigid little mind of yours. Though I suspect that the ice-maiden act is all just a pretence. Is there a real woman in there, Rowan? I'd give the world to find out.'

In spite of her struggles he had taken her in his arms,

planting hot, moist, distasteful kisses on her face and shoulders.

'You'll have to lose that precious virginity some time, sweetheart,' he had muttered thickly. 'Believe me, you don't know what you're missing. Let me——'

And he would have dragged her to the bed if Rowan hadn't lashed out with her hand clenched into a fist, throwing him off balance long enough for her to wrench herself out of his arms and flee to the bathroom, bolting the door securely behind her.

'I suppose I should have told Bernard, asked for his help. But I thought I could handle it. Besides, Colin *is* Bernard's son, and I know he loves him—and it was at this point that we discovered that my mother was ill. She'd been unwell for some time, but now the doctor told us that she had multiple sclerosis. Bernard had enough on his plate. I couldn't burden him with any of my problems.'

If only she had. If only her mother hadn't been ill; then perhaps she would never have got herself into this fix. Rowan shook her head despairingly. It was too late for 'if only'.

'About this time I started seeing Roy.'

Roy. Rowan's face grew white and pinched as she finally spoke his name out loud. The tension of the past days, the stunning impact Nathan had had on her, had pushed thoughts of Roy to the back of her mind, but now they flooded back in full force as Roy's handsome face, dark-haired, blue-eyed, floated before her eyes.

'He worked in the offices of Bernard's firm too, and he was a very attractive man. . .'

She had been attracted to Roy on a personal level, but she had also appreciated the way that seeing him got her out of the house and away from Colin. She had hoped that knowing there was someone else in her life would make her stepbrother leave her alone.

'Roy's big interest was horse-racing. He took me to a couple of meetings, showed me how to put on a bet.'

And that should have warned her, with hindsight she could see that. But it had all seemed just harmless fun at the time. She had even won a pound or two, and Roy had always been very restrained, never risking even as much as a fiver on any race—at least, not when she had been with him.

It had been after one of those trips to the races that Roy had first mentioned his mother. He had been quiet and withdrawn all day, and in the end Rowan had pushed him to tell her what was on his mind. He was worried about his mother, he'd said. She'd lived with him since she'd been widowed three years before, and was totally housebound because she had a weak heart and suffered terribly from arthritis. She couldn't manage the stairs so she was confined to one or two rooms, and she was getting very lonely and depressed.

Looking back, Rowan could see how Roy had been very careful, very clever. He had told her only so much, appearing reluctant to talk about his worries, claiming he didn't want to burden her with them; then he had changed the subject. But he must have known that, with her own mother so ill, she would immediately sympathise with his predicament.

'I liked being with Roy so much because things were very difficult at home.'

Rowan carefully pitched her voice at an objective level, trying hard not to let what she was feeling show through. She had promised Nathan the facts, and the facts were all she should tell him. She could make no excuses, offer no appeals for his sympathy. What she had done was wrong, and it was what she had done that she must confess. Nathan would have no interest in Roy's part in all this.

'And I don't just mean Colin. Bernard was under a lot of strain because the firm was in a slump—jobs weren't coming in and money was getting very tight, and of course he was trying to keep that from my mother so as not to worry her.'

Rowan risked a glance at the man at her side, blue

eyes locking with deep grey for a brief, intent moment before she dropped her gaze to stare down at her rapidly cooling coffee. Nathan's own mug still stood, ignored, on the table, and Rowan wished he would pick it up, drink from it—anything that would give her a few seconds' relief from that searching, dark-eyed scrutiny. Belatedly she regretted her impetuous injunction that he was not to speak. His watchful silence was beginning to prey on her nerves, especially as she was now coming to the most difficult part of her story. Drawing a deep breath, she forced herself to go on.

'At the end of the month I was going through the accounts when I noticed a discrepancy. At first I thought it was just a mistake—after all, I hadn't been doing the books for very long. Before Bernard gave me the job Roy had always seen to them. But when I checked I found that the money was still missing. By now I was really worried—so, naturally, I went to Roy for help.'

'Naturally.' Something had got the better of Nathan's determination to keep strictly to her instructions not to speak as he echoed the word sardonically, and Rowan was disturbed by the harshness of his tone. Did he suspect what was coming? Could he, from a distance, see what, caught up in things emotionally, she had been unable to detect herself?

'Roy seemed very concerned, and we went through the books together, coming up with the same answer— that there was some money missing. But then it began to dawn on me that there was only one person who could have taken it.'

She heard Nathan's indrawn breath hiss between his teeth and nodded miserably.

'That person was Roy.'

The quaver in Rowan's voice revealed how she had felt as the truth came home to her. Roy was the only person with access to the firm's finances other than herself and her stepfather—and Bernard had been working desperately hard, trying to find new customers to keep the men he employed in work, so had left everything up to her. She drew in another deep breath.

'Eventually Roy admitted what he'd done—but he'd been desperate, he'd said, he'd only borrowed the money temporarily.'

'And you believed him?' Nathan's tone told her that she had been all sorts of a fool, but she didn't need anyone else to drive home the message of just how blindly trusting she had been.

But she *had* believed Roy, and she'd understood his reasons for taking the money—or, at least, the reasons he had given her. For a moment she was tempted to tell Nathan those reasons in self-defence, but she had promised herself that she would make no excuses, plead no extenuating circumstances, but face up to what she had done fair and square, and so she caught the words back.

Besides, Nathan, the man whom George had described as 'straight as they come', would probably never be convinced by Roy's tale as she had been. He had already made plain the contempt he felt for her, so why make matters any worse?

'I believed him,' she said flatly.

Roy had sounded so convincing. He had played on her sympathy, telling her that he had bought a bunga-low so that his mother could be more comfortable, but that it needed extensive repairs to make it comfortable and the mortgage had taken every penny he had. His mother had only her pension, so she hadn't been able to help, and because she had been confined to the house there were huge heating bills, special foods, so many expenses to be met that in the end he hadn't known where to turn. 'I know I've been an idiot, Ro,' he'd said with every sign of sincere penitence. 'But I was desperate—I just wasn't thinking straight. Look, if you could just give me twenty-four hours I'll see the bank manager first thing tomorrow—I'm sure they'll let me have a loan, and I can repay the money then with no one any the wiser.'

'You bloody little fool.'

Rowan knew she couldn't deny Nathan's accusation, but then, of course, Roy had known exactly what he'd been doing. He had won her sympathy for his mother already, and, putting herself in his place, she could imagine how hard things would have been for her if Bernard hadn't come into her life. Then she would have been in much the same position as Roy, and she had no idea how she would have managed to support and care for her mother on the wages she earned.

'Yes.' Rowan's voice was very low. 'You're right, but I didn't see that—at least, not at the time. I agreed to cover things up for twenty-four hours, make it look as if the money had been repaid, and he said he'd have the money by then—he *promised*. . .' Her voice broke on the word, and when she continued her tone was dull and full of echoes of the shock that had hit her the next morning. 'When I arrived at the office the next day, the place was alive with gossip. Roy had disappeared—and that was when I learned that he'd run up huge gambling debts and been threatened with prosecution if he didn't pay them.'

The story of his invalid mother had all been a lie, too. Both Roy's parents were still alive and well and living in a small Scottish village.

'I don't know if he took the money to pay his debts or if he'd always intended to run off. Either way, once he knew I'd discovered what he'd done, he'd gone.'

Rowan flashed a quick glance at Nathan's rock-hard face, then wished she hadn't, her eyes skittering away again to stare at a patch of carpet near her feet.

'How much did friend Roy "borrow"?'

Rowan winced at the satirical emphasis on that 'borrow'. 'Over five thousand pounds.'

'And Colin found out, I presume?'

'Yes.'

Rowan's voice sank even lower, to a thin thread of sound that Nathan must have strained to hear.

'I was in a complete panic. I was terrified that

Bernard would find out what I'd done—the way I'd betrayed his trust in me. And Mum had been rather better lately—I was scared that she'd have a relapse if she was told. I went back to my office. . .'

Was it really such a short time ago—barely three days? She felt as if she had lived through a hundred lifetimes since that dreadful day.

'And Colin was there. He had the firm's bank statement and was checking through it—checking it against my records.'

Rowan's voice faltered as the horror of that moment came back to her, the way she had frozen in the doorway, watching Colin ticking off items, knowing he would inevitably find the inaccuracies in her book-keeping. Her hands clenched convulsively as she relived the moment that he had heard her and had turned, that terrible, gloating triumph on his face.

'Well, well, who's been a naughty girl, then?' he had drawled sneeringly.

It had been no good pretending that she didn't know what he meant; the evidence had been there on the desk before her, every entry in her own handwriting, so why should anyone have believed that Roy had had anything to do with it?

'It isn't what you think, Colin. . .'

She had blurted out the whole story, not caring if he believed her.

'So that's what's been happening. You and your boyfriend have been enjoying yourself on the firm's money.'

'No, I never saw any of it. Roy——'

Colin's expletive had dismissed Roy summarily. 'Roy's gone and he's left you to carry the can for him. Embezzlement is a serious crime, and your part in all this makes you an accessory—as guilty as he is.'

'But I'll pay it back—every penny—I promise!'

'Five thousand pounds? Where will you find that sort of money before the annual audit?'

'I don't know—but I'll try. Oh, please, Colin, please don't tell Bernard about this!'

Suddenly and totally unexpectedly Colin's expression had changed, becoming, disturbingly, almost gentle, a smile softening his narrow lips.

'Well, we all make mistakes. How about if I give you a second chance, little sister?'

Rowan hadn't been able to believe what she'd been hearing, her eyes widening in disbelief and desperate hope as they'd gone to her stepbrother's face.

'Do you mean. . .?'

'I can let you have the money to cover this loss. If you put it in the bank today, no one will ever know what happened. If they ask any awkward questions I'll say I used it—make up some feasible story.'

'You'd do that—for *me*?'

Rowan's head had been reeling with relief and the shock of discovering that, after all, Colin had a better side to his nature.

'I'll pay back something out of my wages every month, I promise. Oh, Colin, how can I ever thank you?'

That smile had widened, become a wicked, gloating grin, and a cold shaft of terror had struck home in Rowan's heart as, too late, she'd realised the trap into which she had fallen.

'I'll find a way,' Colin had assured her softly. 'A favour for a favour. If you play your cards right, you won't even have to pay me a penny.'

Nathan's sudden movement at her side recalled Rowan to the present, bringing home to her the fact that, while lost in her memories, she had been pouring out her story automatically.

'You don't have to tell me, I can guess just what the "favour" he wanted was.'

'He wanted me to go to bed with him.' Saying the words out loud made the nightmare more real, and Rowan shuddered violently as she spoke. 'If I did, he'd repay the money, square it so that Bernard wouldn't

realise what had happened, and Mum would never
know a thing. If not——'

'He'd go straight to your stepfather with the whole
story.' Rowan flinched from the bite in Nathan's voice.
'One night with you was worth *five thousand pounds* to
him?'

'It wasn't just *one* night he had in mind.' Rowan's
tone was sharp. The emphasis Nathan had put on that
'five thousand pounds' had stung painfully. Was he
trying to imply that, in his opinion, she wasn't worth
so much?

'But you didn't take him up on the offer?'

'What do you think I am?' Driven past embarrassment, or even fear, Rowan rounded on Nathan
furiously, her blue eyes flashing fire as they met the
coolly assessing darkness of his grey ones. 'I may be
every kind of a fool, but I'm nobody's whore!'

'That wasn't what I said,' Nathan put in quietly,
defusing her anger in a second, leaving her feeling flat
and deflated. He was still there, still listening, something she found very hard to believe. She had been so
sure that when he knew the truth he would reject her
violently. 'So what *did* you do?'

'I panicked. I couldn't think of anything beyond the
fact that I had to get out of there—get away from
Colin and his threats. I just grabbed my bag and ran—
got in my car and drove, not caring where I went. I
didn't even stop to think that I might need money and
clothes, I just wanted to put as many miles as possible
between myself and Colin.'

'Didn't you realise that you were playing right into
Colin's hands? Bullies only win if you let them; they
can't do anything if you stand up to them. By running
away like that, you were admitting guilt——'

'But I *was* guilty—I *am guilty*! And by now Bernard
and my mother know that, too.'

And now *you* know, she added silently. What was
Nathan going to do about what she'd told him? Her
hands clenched on her belt again, nerves stretching

taut as she waited for his reaction. When it came it wasn't at all what she had expected.

'As your stepbrother said, we all make mistakes,' he murmured quietly. 'You've been a bloody irresponsible fool, but——'

He broke off abruptly, looking deep into Rowan's face, and seeing the shadows that still lingered there. At once his eyes narrowed suspiciously.

'Is that it?' he demanded. 'Have you remembered everything?'

That dreadful 'remembered' closed Rowan's throat against the final confession she had to make. 'I—didn't *remember* it,' she managed. For one glorious moment as she spoke the words, she saw in her mind the wall of lies she had built around herself crashing to the ground in a heap of dust and the incredible feeling of freedom that brought gave her the strength to go on. 'I hadn't forgotten any of this. I never lost my memory at all.'

And then, at last, she saw the change in his face that she had dreaded from the beginning.

'You lied to me!' he flung at her from between clenched teeth.

'No—yes—I'm sorry!'

She had said that so many times over the past two days, but this was the hardest, the most difficult. After all he had done for her, her apology was woefully inadequate, but it was all she could manage.

'You're *sorry*?' The sudden flare of emotion in Nathan's eyes made Rowan shrink away in fear that he might actually hit her, but instead he released her arms with an abrupt, rough movement as if just to touch her offended him, and, getting to his feet, he swung away violently, moving to the window to stand staring out at the darkened garden, his hands clenched at his sides and his shoulders tightly hunched as if as a defence against her.

She had known that this would happen, but that didn't make the pain any less. Rowan folded her arms

tightly round herself, rocking backwards and forwards
in her seat in the instinctive comforting movement of a
small, distressed child. But there was no comfort to be
found. She had brought this on herself. She had only
herself to blame, and all she could do was face the
consequences of her actions.

'Nathan. . .' Her voice was just a weak, broken
croak. 'Nathan, say something, please!'

She heard his savagely muttered expletive before he
swung round again and, looking into his face, for a
moment she scarcely recognised him. His skin seemed
almost transparent, it was drawn so tightly across his
cheekbones, and white marks of fury were etched
around his nose and mouth.

'Say something?' he echoed with black cynicism.
'What the hell do you expect me to say? You come
here—break into my life—with some story about being
lost and needing help, claiming you've lost your
memory—and I believed you! I took you in——'

Suddenly seeming to reconsider what he had been
about to say, he broke off violently, slamming the fist
of one hand into the palm of the other with a vicious-
ness that made Rowan flinch away instinctively.

'I wanted to help you,' he went on in a low, harsh
voice that she found infinitely more disturbing than his
former savage anger. 'I would have done anything I
could to help you find out about yourself—but it was
all just a lie! When I saw you that first morning,
on my——'

Once more he broke off, shaking his dark head as if
in despair at the ease with which he had been taken in,
and Rowan knew that there was no need for him to go
on. 'On my wedding day,' he had been about to say,
and nothing could have brought home to her more
forcefully how appallingly she had behaved towards
him than the sight of this man who had always seemed
so sure of things, so completely in control of himself,
now totally at a loss for words.

Suddenly, searingly, she thought she knew how

Nathan was feeling. Hadn't she felt just this way when she had realised how Roy had deceived her and used her? Or wasn't that purely wishful thinking? stern realism forced her to ask herself. After all, she had cared for Roy, at least; to Nathan she was just a stranger, someone he had taken pity on like a stray dog he had found wandering the streets.

'You won't want me to stay now.' Rowan exerted every ounce of control she possessed over her voice, but still it quavered weakly as she got to her feet. 'I'll get dressed and go.'

She had almost reached the door when Nathan's voice, icy cold and bitingly hostile, stopped her dead in her tracks.

'Where the hell do you think you're going?'

'I don't know.' She couldn't find the strength to turn and face him. 'But I can't stay here. You can't want me to stay—not after the way I've treated you. The only thing I can do is get out of your life——'

'You're not going anywhere.'

That had her swinging round, weary resignation clouding her eyes as she faced the fact that of course he wouldn't let her go, not after all she had told him.

'I understand. You want to hand me over to the police—and you're right, of course. That's what any honest person would do. I've committed a crime—I know that—and I should be punished for it. All right, I'll go with you to the police, and I'll tell them everything, just as I've told you. You were right, running away doesn't solve anything. I have to face up to what I've done.'

She wished Nathan would speak instead of staring at her in that blank, unfocused way, almost as if he were seeing straight through her. She'd meant what she'd said. She would go with him to the police station or to face Bernard, whatever he decided.

'Who said anything about the police?'

Nathan's low-voiced question was the last thing she had expected, and for a long moment all she could do was stare back at him in stunned silence. Then at last she found her voice.

'But surely that's what you're going to do?'

'Damn you, Rowan, I don't know what I'm going to do!'

Nathan raked a hand savagely through his dark hair, and weakly Rowan let her eyes follow the movement, unable to stop herself from recalling how it had felt to have those silky strands under her fingertips just a few minutes before—but never, ever again.

Nathan drew a long, uneven breath.

'Go to your room, Rowan,' he commanded, his eyes as hard as stone. 'Go there and stay there. I don't want to see you for a while—I can't think when you're here. When I decide what I'm going to do I'll tell you. Until then, I suggest you try and get some sleep.'

Sleep? Rowan thought despairingly. How could she ever hope to sleep after this? But there was nothing she could say, nothing Nathan would listen to, and, although she had known that it would hurt, she would never have believed how much anguish his rejection of her could bring.

Unhappily she recalled her dreams that one day Nathan might number her among his friends—blind, foolish, impossible dreams, she acknowledged now as, moving with the slow, dragging steps of total mental exhaustion, her whole body sagging despondently, she turned towards the door.

'And don't even consider running away again.' Nathan's voice came from behind her, each word like a knife of ice, stabbing deep into her already desolated heart. 'Because if you do, I swear I'll hunt you out wherever you go—and I'll find you, because there's no place on this earth where you can hide from me.'

CHAPTER SEVEN

WITH a weary sigh Rowan drew the car to a halt and switched off the engine. It was late, well past midnight, and she had been driving for hours after a draining, emotionally exhausting day on top of a virtually sleepless night—and she still had Nathan to face.

A worried, apprehensive frown creased her forehead as she surveyed the house before her, noting the single light that burned in one of the downstairs rooms. Nathan was there—waiting for her, she assumed—and she had no idea just what he wanted from her.

Rowan sighed again, then grimaced in distaste as she caught a glimpse of herself in the driving mirror. She looked a mess, she thought ruefully, Alexa Kennedy's red T-shirt and flowered skirt creased and grubby after hours in the car, her short black hair limp and lifeless in the heat, lying flatly around her pale face, with blue bruises of exhaustion showing under her eyes. Still, that was hardly surprising. After all, it had been a long and very stressful day.

Her mind went back to the moment, earlier that morning, when she had parked the car outside her stepfather's building yard. Her mood had been one of nervous uncertainty and she had been forced to reflect on the difference between the way she now approached Bernard's—and, formerly, her—workplace and the sense of pride and belonging that had always filled her previously. Her job might not be the most important, the most high powered in the world, but it had been *hers*, and along with it had come the knowledge that she was trusted and relied on and that Bernard regarded her as part of his family. Now, very likely, all that was going to change.

Her stomach tangling into tight knots of unease, she

got out of the car, her steps uneven and uncertain as she crossed the pavement. She didn't know how she was going to get through this; she only knew that she had to do it. It was the only way she could put the past behind her and have a chance of beginning again.

Beginning again. The words echoed inside her head with a bitter irony because, deep down, she knew that whatever happened between herself and Bernard there was one way she could never start afresh, and that was with Nathan. A tiny sobbing gasp escaped her as she pictured Nathan's face as she had seen it that morning when she had finally plucked up enough courage to emerge from her room. His expession had been granite hard, the dark eyes hooded and unrevealing, the shadows under them matching those on her own face, clear evidence of the fact that he too had had little sleep during what had remained of the night, and when he'd spoken it had been in such a fiendishly icy, controlled voice that she could only begin to guess at the anger and contempt he was ruthlessly suppressing.

'Afternoon, Rowan.'

A cheery greeting jolted her out of her unhappy reverie, and for a moment she stared blankly at the round, weather-beaten face in front of her before recognition of her stepfather's foreman dawned.

'Oh—hello, Bill,' she managed in uncertain response, not knowing how far the story of her dishonesty had spread. 'Is—is Bernard around?'

'In his office, I think,' the foreman supplied, disconcerting her completely by adding, 'How's your friend?'

'My—friend?'

Bill nodded. 'The one you've been to see in hospital. Nothing serious, I hope?'

'Oh—no.'

It was hard to find the words to answer him. Who had circulated the story that her absence had been because of a visit to a sick friend? Not Colin, surely? As soon as he had realised that his blackmailing scheme hadn't succeeded he must have gone straight to his father to tell him everything. So it must be Bernard who had covered her disappearance in this way.

Rowan's heart felt as if it had been wrenched in two. Even though he now knew the truth about her, Bernard clearly couldn't bear to think that all his workforce should know it too, and he had made up this story to explain her sudden disappearance. Tears of distress and shame burned in her eyes, so that the familiar corridor was just a blur as she made her way to her stepfather's office.

She didn't bother to knock, knowing that even the momentary wait for Bernard to give her permission to come in would eat away at her resolve, but pushed the door open hastily before her nerve could break, then stood staring in shock and horror at the man inside the room.

'Colin!'

'Good morning, Rowan,' her stepbrother returned smoothly. 'So the prodigal's returned—and just in time, too. It was getting a little difficult to maintain the fiction that you were off visiting a friend. Bernard was beginning to get rather anxious, particularly when you didn't phone.'

'Bernard——' Rowan couldn't believe what she was hearing. The words sounded in her ears, but they didn't seem to make any sort of sense. 'Bernard doesn't know?'

Colin shook his head, the gloating smile she detested hovering around his lips.

'You—*you* told him I'd gone to see a friend?'

But why? she wondered as he nodded his head. Why should *Colin* give her a second chance?

'It was the best I could do on the spur of the moment. You see, I knew you'd come to your senses in the end, little sister. I knew you'd come crawling back, needing my help after all. And here you are. It took a little longer than I expected, but——'

'No!'

The thought that Colin believed she had come back to agree to his despicable bargain after all rose like bile in Rowan's throat, leaving a foul, bitter taste. Now, finally, she saw how blindly foolish she had been to believe that she could ever hope to run away from her problems. To do so was just to put the ball right into Colin's court. If she had had the courage to face her mistakes from the start she would never have found herself in this mess.

But in that case she would never have met Nathan, and in spite of everything, in spite of knowing that Nathan now felt nothing but scorn and contempt for her, and no matter how things between herself and Bernard turned out in the end, knowing Nathan, even for such a very brief time, was something she could never regret.

The thought of Nathan made her remember how he had told her that bullies only win if you let them, that the only way to handle them was to face things squarely. The memory was like a sudden surge of energy into her mind. It was almost as if Nathan himself were standing beside her, a source of strength and support, and with a new-found confidence she drew herself up, her chin lifting defiantly as she looked straight into Colin's face.

'I haven't come for your help, Colin. In fact, I haven't come to talk to you at all. It's Bernard I've come to see. Where is he?'

'Right here,' a deep and dearly familiar voice said behind her.

In the moment before she turned Rowan saw the change on Colin's face, saw the gloating triumph fade to be replaced by a red flush of anger, and with a jolt of shock she recognised that mixed with that anger was an admission of defeat. But then her hands were taken in a firm, work-roughened grip and all thought of Colin faded from her mind as she met her stepfather's concerned brown eyes.

'Rowan, it's good to see you. I was worried when

Col said you'd gone off in a rush like that. What happened? How's your friend?'

For a split second Rowan's courage almost deserted her, but then, in the back of her mind, she heard Nathan's voice once more and knew that she could never let him, or herself, down again with any form of dishonesty. Instinctively her hands tightened on Bernard's, because this might be the last time he would ever let her touch him in this way.

'There wasn't any friend, Bernard,' she said firmly.

Behind her she heard Colin mutter a low, obscene curse and a moment later he pushed past her roughly and hurried out of the room. Rowan barely saw him go, her attention concentrated on the man before her.

'I've something to tell you, Bernard—something I'm desperately ashamed of, but I want you to know the truth.'

She might have thought that, having told the story once, to Nathan, it would be easier the second time, but in fact Rowan found it very much harder because as she spoke she could again see Nathan's face as he had listened to the same story, his intent concentration, the darkening of his eyes as he had realised where her tale was heading, and the final, savage withdrawal at the end. So it took many false starts, broken sentences and awkward repetitions before everything was said and she stood silent again, waiting for her stepfather to speak. But once it was out she felt so much better, drained and exhausted, still thoroughly ashamed, but cleaner, and somehow refreshed, as if the whole process had been a form of exorcism.

This was why she had known she had had to come back, why that morning when, in response to her nervous enquiry about what he was going to do, Nathan had stunned her with the harsh question, 'What do *you* want to do?' she had found herself answering clearly and confidently. 'I want to go home and tell Bernard the truth—the whole truth. I'm the one who did wrong and I should be the one to tell him so.'

Not for a moment had she believed, or even allowed herself to hope, that Nathan would let her do any such thing, so his swift response had rocked her sense of reality, making her feel as if she had lost her grip on the world she lived in.

'Then that's what you'll do. Your car's ready—I had the tank filled up with petrol yesterday. That should see you home.'

'Rowan——' Bernard's voice, low and shaken, broke into her thoughts. 'Oh, Rowan, why didn't you come to me before things got to this stage—when you first found out about Roy?'

'I was blind.' Rowan brushed at her eyes with the back of her hand. 'And I believed his story.' With Bernard, there had been no holding back; she had told him everything, all the details she hadn't dared reveal to Nathan. 'I couldn't help putting myself in his place and thinking how I'd feel with Mother so ill and no chance of providing the comforts she needed. I'm afraid I didn't stop to think about what it might do to you. Oh, Bernard, can you ever forgive me.'

The sound of a clock striking the half-hour brought Rowan back to the present, making her realise that she had been sitting, lost in thought, for almost a quarter of an hour. Nathan must have heard her arrive, but he hadn't come out to her. He was waiting for her to go to him—if she could find the mental strength to move.

It was a struggle. Every muscle ached with a fatigue that was more than physical, and her mind seemed incapable of further thought. She felt as if she had been away for weeks instead of hours, a feeling that was aggravated by a terrible sense of loneliness and desolation, which was strange when, logically, it would have been more natural for her to have been experiencing a wonderful sense of release.

Because Bernard had forgiven her. In his generous-spirited way, he had understood that she had never actually set out to help Roy defraud him and that she

had acted crazily, blindly, but not deliberately criminally. He had accepted her promise that she would pay
back every penny of the money Roy had taken—with
interest—and had adamantly refused to inform the
police of Roy's actions because to do so would incrim-
inate Rowan herself. The only time his gentle understanding had wavered had been when she had told him
that she couldn't stay, that she had to go back to
Farmworth House—and Nathan—that night.

'But *why*, Rowan? I don't understand. Who is this
man? What sort of a hold does he have over you?'

'It's not like that, Bernard.'

Rowan had spoken wearily, unable to explain to her
stepfather that the real hold Nathan had over her was
the fact that she had deceived him in a way that was
perhaps even worse than the way she had covered up
Roy's theft from Bernard, worse than the way Roy had
treated her, and she couldn't run away from the
consequences of her behaviour. She had ruined
Nathan's life, destroyed his marriage plans, so she
owed him whatever compensation he might demand in
return.

'He was good to me, and he helped me so much. I
don't know what I would have done without him. And
he made me promise that when I'd seen you I'd go
back.'

That was something Bernard hadn't been able to
understand, and, Rowan admitted to herself as she got
out of the car, neither could she. She climbed the steps
to the door and pressed the bell automatically, her
mind still full of the last minutes before she had left for
Carborough.

'Then that's what you'll do,' Nathan had said, and
she hadn't been able to believe that he had meant that
she was free to go.

'But what about you?'

'Me?' Her question seemed to have taken Nathan
aback, his own coming sharply in response.

'I mean—aren't you going to report me to the police?'

Something in what she had said seemed to have angered him, the dark frown that settled over his features being distinctly disturbing.

'That's up to your stepfather,' he declared curtly. 'He's the injured party. If he wants to press charges, that's his decision.'

And one he wanted no part of, his tone implied only too clearly, Rowan acknowledged on the wave of dark misery. If he had intended to press home the fact that he wanted nothing more to do with her, he couldn't have made it more plan if he'd tried. She'd expected this, had known it must come if she told him the truth, but that didn't make the pain any easier to bear. There was a raw, bleeding hole where her heart should be at the thought that this would be the last time she would ever see Nathan Kennedy. Once she was home— whatever happened there—their paths were never likely to cross again, and even in the unlikely event of that happening Nathan would want nothing to do with her, would probably not even acknowledge her existence.

Through the anguish that clouded her mind she heard Nathan speak, but his words didn't register on her brain.

'I'm sorry—what did you say?'

Nathan's breath hissed sharply between his teeth before he repeated his statement slowly and clearly.

'I said—there's a condition.'

Of course. She had taken so much from him; it was only natural he would want repayment.

'I'll pay back everything you've spent on me—the petrol, my food. Just as soon as I get home I'll send you a cheque—and I'll have Alexa's clothes cleaned and sent back——'

'That isn't what I meant!'

Rowan couldn't understand Nathan's tone. On the surface he sounded harshly angry, but underneath that there was an inexplicable raw note that roughened his voice.

'Wha—what else do you want?'

'If things go all right with your stepfather—even if he doesn't want to take this matter any further, I do. When he lets you go I want you to promise you'll come back here.'

In a catalogue of unbelievable shocks, this was the most unexpected, and Rowan had to reach out a hand to a nearby chair to support herself as the ground seemed to rock beneath her feet.

'But why? I don't understand!'

What had she said to bring that darkness to his eyes, the frighteningly bitter twist to his mouth?

'No, I don't suppose you do,' Nathan returned sardonically. 'I'm not all that sure I understand myself—but that's my condition for letting you go. Either you give me your word that when you have things sorted out at home—however long that takes— you'll come back here, or you don't go at all.'

'But I have to go!'

Through the haze of confusion that filled her mind that one thing was clear. She *had* to see Bernard, had to face up to what she had done. She couldn't see any possible reason why Nathan should want her to stay, unless it was as some form of revenge for the way she had lied to him and used him. It was a savage irony that only minutes before she had been desolate at the thought of never seeing him again and now he was demanding that she did—but in such a way that she didn't know if she could bear it.

'Nathan, I *have* to see Bernard. I have to put things right with him.'

'Then you'll give me your word that you'll come back,' Nathan declared, his voice and expression stonily adamant, leaving her no choice but to give the promise he demanded. . .

'So you came back.'

For a second Rowan thought that the voice she

heard was still part of her memories, but then, realising that the door had opened, the light from the hall spilling out on to the steps, she turned wide, apprehensive eyes on the tall, strong figure standing in the doorway.

'I gave my word,' she managed shakily, cursing the fact that the light was behind him, leaving his face in shadow, as impenetrable as the night around them so that she could gain no clue to his mood.

'So you did.' It was spoken in a flat monotone, unrevealing of any feeling. Nathan took a step backwards, opening the door wider. 'You'd better come in.'

If she had been walking into a lion's den she couldn't have felt any more afraid, Rowan thought, her mouth drying and her heart starting to pound unevenly so that her steps were unsteady as she moved into the hall. Her feelings were aggravated by a rush of heightened awareness of Nathan's forceful physical attraction as she saw him in the full light at last, her eyes moving greedily over the firm lines of his body in the navy shirt and trousers he wore. She felt as if she had been starved of the sight of him, even after only a few hours, the beat of her heart sounding like the pounding of heavy waves in her ears as she admitted to herself that, after all, the promise he had extracted from her had been irrelevant. She would never have been able to stay away. No matter what the consequences, she would have had to see Nathan just once more.

'Have you eaten?' Nathan asked gruffly.

'No—I didn't dare stop on the way or it would have been almost dawn before I got here.'

She didn't add that she couldn't have swallowed anything if she'd tried, that her throat had been so tense, her stomach so twisted into tight, painful knots that to eat a single thing would have been an impossibility. She had broken the speed limit to get back by this time, her foot pressed down hard on the accelerator so that her car had sped towards its destination like a homing pigeon flying to its roost.

But this wasn't her home. She didn't belong here—in fact, she doubted if she was even wanted, to judge by the stiff, distant mask that was Nathan's face. But in that case *why* had he insisted that she return? Rowan abandoned the problem as insoluble. Nathan would tell her what he had in mind when he was ready.

'But I'm not hungry,' she added hastily to forestall the offer of food that Nathan was clearly about to make. If she hadn't been able to face the prospect of eating on the journey, then she certainly couldn't do so now. 'Except—perhaps—I would like a drink.'

She would need something to help her face whatever was coming—though what that was she had no way of knowing. Nathan hadn't insisted on her return simply for the pleasure of her company, that much was certain.

'I made some fresh coffee when I heard your car.'

The oblique reference to the fact that he was well aware of the way she had been sitting outside for some time stretched Rowan's already taut nerves even tighter as she followed Nathan towards the living-room.

'It should be ready by now.'

The coffee was clearly not the first Nathan had made that night if the evidence of the half-full mugs standing at various points around the room was anything to go by. It seemed as if he had been constantly pouring himself a drink and then forgetting it, leaving it to grow cold where it stood, something that was so much at odds with the meticulous tidiness Rowan had noticed during her brief stay that it caused her to study Nathan's face more closely.

He looked tired, she reflected sadly, tired and drawn, with lines of strain etched around his nose and mouth, and those deep grey eyes were shadowed and clouded. He was in need of a shave, stubble showing darkly around his jaw, and his hair was tousled as if he had frequently pushed his hands through it in the gesture of unease she had seen many times before.

Had he been thinking about Meryl and his lost

happiness? A bitter pain stabbed deep in Rowan's heart at the thought that, without the distraction of her own unwanted presence, Nathan must have had time to face the full fact of his loss. Had he spent the whole day brooding about the woman he had loved and lost, perhaps trying to get in touch with her—unsuccessfully, to judge by the way he looked now?

That thought made her legs suddenly as weak as cotton wool, unable to support her, and she sank hastily and inelegantly into the nearest chair, snatching at the coffee-cup Nathan held out to her and sipping at it unthinkingly, needing something to ease the sudden cold that seemed to have turned her blood to ice in her veins. She had to choke back a cry of pain as she burned her tongue savagely as a result.

'Steady!'

It was a mild, even gentle reproof, nothing threatening in it, but the tone in which it was uttered was the one Rowan remembered as belonging to the old Nathan, the man she had known before this coldly distant stranger had taken his place, and so it drove a burning knife into her heart with the thought that never again could things be as they had been then.

'I'm—all right.'

A curt nod was Nathan's only response as he took his own cup and moved to the chair opposite, just as he had done on the night when she had told him the truth. Dear God, was it really less than twenty-four hours ago?

'You saw your stepfather.'

There was something strange about Nathan's intonation, something that jarred on Rowan's nerves, but, unable to pin-point exactly what it was, she could only answer him simply.

'Yes, I saw him.'

'And you've sorted everything out.'

'Yes. Bernard——'

'Isn't going to press charges. He's willing to let you pay back the money and forget the whole thing.'

With a blinding sense of disorientation it dawned on Rowan just what it was that had seemed strange about the way Nathan had spoken. He wasn't asking questions, he was stating facts. He *knew* what had happened between herself and Bernard!

'Why are you asking me this? You know what happened—but how?'

Nathan didn't answer, but a tiny flicker of his eyes towards the telephone gave him away.

'You *rang* Bernard!'

He made no attempt to deny it, a swift tightening of the hand that held his coffee-cup the only indication of any reaction to her accusation.

'You were checking up on me!'

Rowan shivered as the full force of those dark eyes was turned on her face.

'Wouldn't you?' The sardonic inflexion made her wince. 'After all, your behaviour has hardly been the sort that would inspire unquestioning trust.'

And there was nothing she could say in her own defence in response to that, because she couldn't deny that Nathan had only spoken the truth.

'When did you ring him?' she asked in a lower voice.

Briefly Nathan consulted his watch. 'About three hours ago. I wanted to make sure you'd had plenty of time to get there and talk things out.'

'But why? Why did you do it? And if you were going to check on me that way, why did you insist that I came back here? I don't understand any of this.'

'I wanted you to come back for one very particular reason.'

Nathan blatantly ignored Rowan's first two questions, concentrating on the third. For a long moment he stared down into the dark liquid in his cup, his face set in lines of total impassivity.

'I have a small problem at work,' he went on with such a total *non sequitur* that Rowan could hardly believe she had heard him right. 'My secretary is having a baby. She was due to take maternity leave

from August, but apparently there are some compli-
cations and the doctor has insisted that she gives up
work immediately in order to rest. That leaves me
rather in the lurch.'

Was she going crazy, Rowan wondered, or was
Nathan? What possible relevance could his secretary's
health have to the present situation? She felt as if she
had learned her lines in a play only to discover that the
rest of the cast were working from a completely
different script.

'I don't see what this has to do with me.'

The gaze Nathan turned on her was frighteningly
blank. She felt as if he were looking straight through
her, as if she didn't even exist.

'I have no replacement for Eve,' he went on
smoothly, as if he hadn't heard her interjection, 'which
could be a problem—so that is where you come in.'

'*Me?*'

Nathan nodded slowly. 'You're a trained secretary—
experienced, too—and you've worked in the construction business with your stepfather. I want you to take
Eve's place until she's ready to return to work.'

'To take——You dragged me all the way back here
to offer me a *job*?'

Nathan inclined his head slightly and his smile wasn't
one Rowan liked at all, the way it didn't touch his eyes
sending a shiver of apprehension down her spine.

'Not *offer*,' he corrected levelly. 'You are taking the
job, Rowan, and that's all there is to it.'

She couldn't! She couldn't work with him, knowing
what he thought of her. She couldn't bear to be so very
close to him every day and yet be so terribly, devastatingly far away.

'I won't do it! I already have a job—with Bernard. I
owe him all that money and I have to pay it back
and——'

'Bernard is willing to let you go,' Nathan put in
quietly, halting her abruptly in mid-flow.

'Bernard is willing. . .' Rowan knew she sounded

like a dazed parrot, repeating everything Nathan said, but she couldn't help herself. This whole situation was totally unbelievable. 'You've already asked him?'

Once again Nathan's dark head tilted to the side in agreement. 'When I put the proposition to him he considered it a very good idea. Naturally, you'll want to pay off your debts as quickly as possible, and I can offer you a much better salary than the one your stepfather was paying you. He won't lose by the deal; I'm in a position to put some very profitable business his way—and now that you don't owe him any-thing——'

'But I do!'

Rowan couldn't go on. She owed Bernard so much, and not just the five thousand pounds Roy had taken from him. But she owed Nathan so much, too—wasn't that why she had come back here in spite of her stepfather's protests? She owed Nathan more than she could ever repay. Without his help she didn't know what she would have done, and it had been his insistence that she had to face up to what she had done that had brought her to the realisation that running away solved nothing. If it hadn't been for Nathan, she might never have gone back to Bernard, might still be running now.

'No—you owe me.' Nathan's clear, precise tones hit her like a blow to her head.

'I owe *you*?' Rowan stared in total bemusement as Nathan nodded slowly.

'About five thousand pounds' worth,' he murmured with deceptive softness.

'What?' Rowan shot bolt upright in her seat, coffee slopping over the side of her cup. 'What are you talking about? I don't owe. . .' Her voice failed as she read the answer in his face and a tidal wave of shock swamped her. 'The money——'

'The money Roy took from your stepfather,' Nathan confirmed with appalling equanimity. 'Bernard's firm is too small and in too precarious a position to sustain a loss like that.'

Dear God, he'd found out everything! How long had he talked to Bernard? Just what had her stepfather told him? And, more importantly, what had *Nathan* said to get Bernard to agree to this idea?

'But to Kennedy Construction it's small change,' Nathan continued imperturbably, though Rowan was sure that those keenly watchful dark eyes had noticed her loss of colour, the way her own eyes had become wide blue pools of shock. 'Your stepfather would have managed somehow—he loves you very much—but it would have caused all sorts of problems. He was relieved, to say the least, when I told him I would refund the money in full if he released you to come and work for me.'

'You told—you'd refund. . .' Rowan's mind seemed to have blown a fuse, so that she was incapable of stringing coherent words together. With a determined effort she got a grip on herself. 'That money is *my* responsibility!'

'Not any more,' Nathan returned with frightening calmness. 'I've paid off your debt to your stepfather. You don't owe him anything—you owe me.'

He paused for a nicely calculated moment to allow his words to sink in, but there was no need. Rowan was only too aware of what he had said—and the possible repercussions to herself of that declaration.

'And, believe me, I intend to get full value for the money I've paid out.'

She had no doubt about that, Rowan reflected unhappily. The problem was that Nathan had no idea just how much, in personal terms, it was going to cost her to repay that debt.

CHAPTER EIGHT

'Do YOU want a lift home, Rowan?'

Rowan glanced up from her desk to smile at the slim, dark-haired figure in the doorway. It wasn't fair, she reflected for perhaps the hundredth time, that Alexa Kennedy should be so obviously Nathan's sister. They were so very alike, Nathan's strong-boned features softened in his sister's face, the glossy dark hair exactly the same shade, their eyes only very slightly different, Alexa's dove-coloured to Nathan's storm-cloud grey. In the twelve weeks she had been working for Kennedy Construction she still hadn't adjusted to the fact that, even when Nathan himself wasn't around, his sister's appearance was a constant, tormenting reminder of his presence.

'I'd love one, but I really should finish here first.'

'Oh, come on!' Alexa protested. 'It's nearly six and you've had your nose to the grindstone all day. Surely even my slave-driver brother couldn't object if you left now? By my reckoning you've done over eight hours' overtime already this week—and it *is* Friday.'

'Slave-driver' was the right word, Rowan admitted to herself. Nathan had said that he intended to get full value for the money he had paid out on her account, and he had proceeded to do exactly that. She had never worked so hard in her life as she had done over the last three months, but deep down she was relieved that things had been that way. The tasks Nathan piled on her filled her working hours, the concentration it required leaving her little time to brood about her situation, and when she finally did get back to the house she was usually too exhausted to do much more than snatch a hasty meal and fall into bed.

'Leave it, Rowan!' Alexa insisted. 'Work will always

be there, but now it's the weekend—two whole days free from the office.'

Rowan had to struggle to suppress the bitter grimace that threatened to cross her face. She couldn't share Alexa's enthusiasm at the prospect of the coming weekend. The two days when she wasn't at work were the most difficult to get through because, inevitably, they meant forty-eight seemingly endless hours spent in Nathan's company without the demands of work to distract her.

She couldn't imagine why, once she had decided to accept the job—a decision which hadn't really been a decision because, as she knew very well, she had had no other choice—Nathan had decreed that instead of finding a flat in Farmworth she should live with him and Alexa at Farmworth House. She had fought against that idea from the start, but Nathan had appeared unmoved by her protests.

'I usually make arrangements to provide temporary accommodation for new employees who have just moved into the area. In your case, seeing as the job itself isn't permanent, my home seems to be the most appropriate and convenient place.'

'Then I insist that we come to some sort of agreement.' Rowan had to make an effort to ensure that the sting of that cold reminder that her place in his life was only temporary didn't show in her voice.

One dark eyebrow lifted in ironic enquiry. 'And what sort of—agreement—did you have in mind?'

Just when she could least handle it, when she most needed to be firmly in control and strictly businesslike, Rowan was assailed by a terrible sense of loss for the Nathan she had first met, the man who it now seemed had gone from her forever, hidden behind this taunting, indifferent mask.

'A *business* agreement.' Her inner pain made the words come out clipped and tight. 'I insist on paying my share of living expenses—heating, lighting, food— and something on top as rent.'

The tightening of the muscles at the corner of Nathan's mouth made her wonder if he was about to point out that she was in no position to insist on anything, but he swiftly converted his reaction into a bland and, Rowan felt, totally insincere smile.

'Do you think you can manage that on top of the repayments of your——' a nicely calculated pause drove his point home '—your debt to me?'

'I'll make sure I do.'

It wouldn't be easy, but she was determined to manage it. She would do without any extras, skimp on meals, even go without visits home, though that would be the hardest thing of all—whatever it took to get the money paid back so that she would be free to live her own life again. What that life would be like, knowing that Nathan was only some hours' drive away and yet never being able to see him, she didn't know, but nothing could be worse than the way she was existing now, seeing him every day and knowing that he despised and detested her for what she had done.

Paying for her living expenses would inevitably mean that she could afford less in the way of repayments which, in turn, would extend the length of time she had to endure the present situation, but she couldn't do it any other way. Her conscience and what was left of her self-respect would leave her no peace if she did.

'I can't live on your charity!' she declared, rather too vehemently to judge from the way Nathan's brows drew together in a frown.

'Not charity, Rowan,' he corrected with deceptive mildness. 'You are helping me out of a difficult situation.'

'And we both know why I'm doing that! You didn't give me any choice in the matter. Personally, I wish I'd gone to some loan shark for the money, even if they did charge a fortune in interest.'

The smile that curled Nathan's mouth was not a pleasant one, sending a shiver down Rowan's spine as she saw the way it had no effect on his eyes, leaving them as cold and hard as chips of grey ice.

'Then it's a pity you didn't think of that in the first place,' he murmured softly, with acid under the silk of his voice. 'It would have saved us both a great deal of trouble.'

The only possible explanation that Rowan could come up with for Nathan's insistence that she stayed at Farmworth House was that, knowing her untrustworthy record, he wanted to have her firmly under his surveillance so that he could watch her every minute of the day. She had only herself to blame for that, but she found every second spent in Nathan's home an agonising torment with its reminders of those early days, before she had admitted the truth, and so, even when Nathan hadn't insisted on official overtime, she had often found an excuse to stay late at her desk in order to minimise the ordeal as much as possible—and she had planned on doing that tonight.

'I really think——' she began, but Alexa was clearly determined to override her protests.

'Work is over for today,' she said firmly, removing the file Rowan had been working on and closing it with a decisive snap. 'Everyone else has gone home, and it's time we did too.'

'I never understood why you sold your car,' Alexa said when the streets of Farmworth had been left behind and they were in the winding country roads that led to the house. 'I would have thought you'd really need it here. It's such a trek into town with buses so few and far between.'

'I needed the money—and I couldn't afford to run it any more.'

Try as she might, Rowan couldn't iron out the unevenness in her voice. She had sold her car as soon as she had moved into Farmworth House, making a loss on the deal as she had known she inevitably would, and had handed the money straight to Nathan in part payment of the amount she owed him. It barely covered a tenth of her debt, but it was a start, and she had felt so much better for doing it.

'But Nathan pays you a decent salary—and if you were really stuck I'm sure he'd consider an advance. You'd only have to ask——'

'No!'

Rowan's reaction had been too swift, too sharp, as the curious glance Alexa shot her told her, but the thought of owing Nathan anything more than she did already was more than she could bear. She couldn't forget his reaction when she had given him the cheque for the money from her car.

'What's this?' he had asked, barely glancing at the slip of paper, his eyes subjecting her to a cold, steely scrutiny that dried her carefully thought-out speech in her throat.

'It's a cheque,' she had muttered inanely.

'*That* I can see,' was the bitingly satirical response, calculated to make her feel less than three inches high—and succeeding only too well.

'It's part of what I owe you.' Completely thrown off balance mentally, she floundered awkwardly. 'It's not as much as I'd like, but it's a beginning.'

Nathan spared the cheque a second, fleeting glance, an ominous frown darkening his face as he registered the figures written on it.

And how did you come by that amount?'

The sardonic question hit home with a force that had Rowan gasping in shock and distress. Nathan actually suspected that she might resort to some underhand means of finding the money she owed him.

'If you must know, I sold my car. . .' The catch in her voice gave too much away, revealing only too clearly how much his dark irony had hurt. 'And it was Roy who stole the money!'

'With your help.'

'I didn't *know*!'

'You didn't know or you didn't want to know?'

Nathan challenged. 'Just what was it about the man that made you trust him so much?'

The question left Rowan floundering for an answer, not because of the way it made her think about her relationship with Roy, but because of the questions it provoked about Nathan himself. She had rushed into trusting Roy because she had needed to believe that all men weren't like her stepbrother. He had seemed gentle, kind and considerate—but she had very soon been disillusioned. His behaviour should have taught her to be wary of believing in any man in the future, but instead she had trusted Nathan, had wanted him as a friend, had come back here as he'd asked, taken this job, without ever questioning his motives. Colin and Roy had both used her for their own ends; why should Nathan be any different?

She suddenly felt desperately cold inside, lost and afraid, so that she couldn't answer Nathan's question with the truth, but dodged round it instead.

'He needed the money, and——'

'And you have such a very generous heart.' Somehow Nathan managed to make what, coming from anyone else, would have been a compliment sound like a scathing condemnation, his darkly satirical tone lashing Rowan so that she flung a response at him without thinking.

'Since when has that been a crime?'

Nathan's smile was unnerving. 'Oh, it isn't. It's just that I find such generosity of spirit rather hard to believe when you've already proved yourself a very convincing liar.'

'What exactly are you trying to say?'

But the question was unnecessary. Rowan already knew the direction in which Nathan's thoughts were heading—knew it and resented it.

'Are you suggesting that what I've told you about Roy is all a pack of lies?'

If the cap fits. . . Nathan didn't actually speak the words; his expression said it all for him. 'Perhaps you and your lover planned it all between you, with you cooking the books to cover up what you'd done. What went wrong, Rowan? Did he run out on you before you were ready?'

'You really think I'd do that—to Bernard?'

'I've only your word that it happened any other way—and evidence of your honesty is rather sparse on the ground.'

Rowan's indignation evaporated in a rush, leaving her limp and deflated like a pricked balloon. There was no answer to that, no way she could deny the way she had lied to him at the beginning, so she had only herself to blame if he thought the worst of her.

But then another, disturbing thought came into her mind. She had wondered if Nathan might be using her, but now his savage attack made her wonder if there might be another side to things. Was it possible that, smarting from the pain of Meryl's rejection on their wedding day, Nathan was taking out his bitterness on the first victim that came to hand because his fiancée wasn't available?

'Bernard is very dear to me. I love him like a father——'

'And yet you haven't been near him or your mother for weeks.'

The injustice of that accusation burned like acid. If only he knew how much she longed to go home, but had determined that even that must be sacrificed to the repayment of her debt to him. She might feel terribly guilty at what she had done, be prepared to do anything to put things right, but she wasn't going to be Nathan's own private whipping-boy, someone he kicked whenever he was feeling down.

'That's none of your damn business! How I live my life is my own affair—it has nothing at all to do with you!'

'You're not exactly keen on my brother, are you?' Alexa's question broke in on Rowan's uncomfortable memories. 'I've noticed how you tense up whenever he speaks to you.'

'I find him——' Rowan hunted for the right word '—difficult to get to know,' she settled for in the end, totally inadequately. 'He's very imposing.'

That wasn't strictly accurate. Devastating summed up her feelings much more closely.

'He can be,' Alexa laughed. 'But that's just his business image. Don't let the big macho man act fool you; deep inside, Nathan's just a great softy with a heart of marshmallow.'

Not the Nathan *she* knew, Rowan reflected privately. That first Nathan, yes, she could have believed Alexa's description of him, but the man he had since become was as hard as iron, through and through.

But then Alexa wasn't likely to have seen the side of her brother that he showed to Rowan. Nathan loved and admired his younger sister, that much was evident in the way he consulted her on staffing problems, always listening intently to her opinions, the teasing comments about her inveterate clothes-buying, which were, nevertheless, always followed by some appreciative comment about the way she looked, and, above all, in the warmth and affection that showed in his face and voice whenever they talked. But of course Alexa had never deceived him, lied to him as Rowan had.

'I should have thought you'd have realised that after living with us all this time.'

That was true, of course. Rowan's heart twisted painfully as she acknowledged that, seeing Nathan at work and in his home every day, it was impossible not to be aware of the finer points of his character—and there were plenty of those to observe. She already knew about his innate generosity, his gentleness, his kindness and sensitive consideration. She had experienced all of them in those first few days that now seemed like a dreamlike idyll which cold reality had totally replaced. But there was much more to Nathan

Kennedy, as she had been discovering over the past three months.

The first thing she had learned was that he was a brilliantly astute businessman with an incisive, clear-thinking mind that could swiftly cut through to the heart of a problem, analyse the possibilities and come up with exactly the right solution. Working with him was more than a job, it was an experience. She had learned an immense amount in the brief time she had been at Kennedy Construction and had been over-whelmed with admiration at what she had seen.

There were other facets to his character, too, some that any casual observer could see, like his unfailing courtesy with even the most difficult people, his sense of fairness, the ease with which he communicated with his workforce, all of whom clearly idolised him and would do anything he asked, and other, more intimate traits that only someone who watched him closely would detect.

And Rowan *did* watch him closely; she couldn't help herself. Even though she knew it was a masochistic form of self-torture, she couldn't stop herself from absorbing every little detail about him, storing it up in her memory as a form of insurance against the time when she would leave Farmworth House and such memories would be all she had left.

She knew that, like her, Nathan loved the gentle hours of the early morning. On the first day of her stay at Farmworth House she had woken at six as she always did and, after getting dressed, had gone down to the garden. Believing herself completely alone, it had come as a jolting shock to hear Nathan's quiet greeting and, spinning round, to discover that he had been sitting in the shade of a huge oak tree, silently observing her.

'I'm sorry,' she said hastily, her voice sounding breathless because of the uneven pounding of her heart. 'I didn't know anyone was here.'

He looked so relaxed, leaning back against the

enormous trunk of the ancient tree, coffee-mug in hand, his hair slightly ruffled, his jaw unshaven, his clothes a casual short-sleeved shirt and denim jeans, the slightly dishevelled look making him appear much more human and infinitely more approachable. In a short time he would go inside, shower and shave, change into one of the impeccably tailored suits that were his normal office wear, and this Nathan would disappear, replaced once more by the sleekly efficient businessman she found so difficult to talk to.

'I like to come out here for an hour or so before starting work,' Nathan said quietly. 'It gives me a chance to wake up slowly, and I enjoy the peace and quiet.'

'I enjoy the peace and quiet.' Softly spoken as the words were, the dismissal implied in them was too pointed to miss, destroying the moment of unspoken empathy in a second.

'I didn't mean to disturb you,' Rowan said stiffly. 'It won't happen again.'

Her heart sank as she saw Nathan's frown, then his shoulders lifted in a dismissive shrug. 'The garden's big enough to hold an army camp,' he said, his tone strangely flat and dull. 'There's plenty of room for both of us.'

Providing you make sure we don't meet, Rowan added miserably in the privacy of her own thoughts, and from then on she always checked from her window to see if Nathan was already up, strictly avoiding the area round the old oak tree so that there was no chance of her intruding on his morning peace ever again.

'We just don't hit it off, Alexa,' she told Nathan's sister jerkily. 'We're incompatible—it happens.'

'Hmm.' Alexa didn't sound convinced. 'Incompatible seems a bit strong to me. I've seen the way Nathan watches you. Sometimes he can't take his eyes off you.'

That was something Rowan couldn't deny. So many times during the past weeks she had been alerted by some sort of sixth sense, a prickle of awareness that

lifted the tiny hairs on the back of her neck, and had
glanced up to find Nathan's dark eyes fixed on her, his
expression sombre, assessing, his mood impossible to
interpret. No, she knew that he watched her, but,
unlike Alexa, she could provide a very different explanation for his scrutiny.

Nathan didn't trust her. He felt nothing but contempt for her, despising and detesting the way she had
behaved, and he watched for some sign that she had
reverted to what he believed were her old, irresponsible ways, some indication that she had betrayed his
trust or deceived him in some way. At times she had
been close to hysteria, the pressure of that constant
surveillance weighing her down so that she had come
near to rounding on him, demanding to know if he
thought that she would run off with the family silver if
he turned his back for a second.

'It can't be easy for him having a stranger living in
his home like this,' she said carefully. She had no idea
what explanation Nathan had given his sister for her
own presence in their home, but whatever he had said
seemed to have satisfied Alexa. From the time she had
arrived back at Farmworth House after her stay with
friends that had resulted from Nathan's ruined wedding
plans she had accepted Rowan unhesitatingly and
without question, offering a friendly welcome that had
been a balm to the younger girl's raw and depressed
spirits.

'Oh, I don't think that would bother Nathan—and I
really don't see why you say you don't get on with him.
It strikes me that you two have a lot in common—your
tastes in music, for example. Nathan's always
despaired of me because I don't appreciate his Bach
and Beethoven, but the two of you can sit for hours,
lost to the world, when it's playing. And look at the
way you both enjoyed that dreary old film last week.'

'That dreary old film was the classic black and white
version of *The Importance of Being Earnest*!' Rowan
protested.

'Well, it bored me rigid,' retorted Alexa, whose tastes, to her brother's disgust, veered towards slick American thrillers.

Nathan himself preferred a much more subtle approach to entertainment, and his delight in the Oscar Wilde play had been something that Rowan could share with him unreservedly. The memory of that night, and of the occasions Alexa had mentioned, when Nathan had played the *St Matthew Passion* or the 'Pastoral' Symphony on his elaborate stereo, had been rare occasions when the barriers of restraint and distance that he normally imposed on their relationship had come down in the face of their mutual pleasure. But then as soon as the film or the record had ended those barriers had gone up again, and it was as if those moments of sharing had never been.

'In fact, as they say, you seem as if you were made for each other.'

'Alexa!' Rowan's protest was low, shaken, her inner feelings in such turmoil that it was a struggle to speak. 'You want to be careful what you say or someone might think you were matchmaking.'

'That's an idea,' Alexa laughed. 'Nathan could do with someone new in his life after Meryl.'

Meryl. Rown shifted uncomfortably in her seat, a prey to a host of disturbing emotions. This was the first time that Nathan's ex-fiancée's name had been mentioned in her hearing since she had moved into Farmworth House. There seemed almost to be a conspiracy of silence around the subject. The other woman might have vanished off the face of the earth, might never have existed, she had been so firmly erased from Nathan's life. Rowan had expected one or two awkward moments, at work perhaps, or when Alexa returned to the house, but nothing had happened. Recalling Nathan's words about his family knowing when it was wiser to keep their distance, she had assumed that he and his sister had some tacit agreement that that painful episode was not to be discussed—something which, in Rowan's opinion, spoke volumes for the way he was feeling even though he let none of those emotions show on the surface.

'I don't think that idea would appeal to your brother,' she said hastily, terrified that Alexa might actually take it up.

It wasn't what she wanted to say. What she really wanted to do was to ask if Alexa knew how her brother was feeling, whether he had contacted Meryl or she him. After the way he had been driving himself—and her—over the past weeks she strongly suspected that Nathan was burying his hurt in his work, pushing himself to the point where, like Rowan, he was too tired to think as his way of dealing with the pain and loss that were the result of his ruined marriage plans.

A low, despondent sigh escaped her at the thought. She had put things right with Bernard and she was working hard to repay the money she owed Nathan. The shame, the guilt at what she had done were still there, but at least she was doing something to put things right. Meryl was a different matter entirely. There was nothing she could do about that.

She *had* tried. When she had first started working at Kennedy Construction, a few, very discreet enquiries had obtained Meryl's full name and the address of the offices of her design company. Secretly she had called at those offices and rung them as often as she'd dared, wanting to explain what had happened, to plead with the other woman and beg her to forgive Nathan and give him another chance. But each time her enquiries had met with the same unhelpful response. Miss Freeman wasn't in the office. She was away on holiday and they had no idea when she would be back.

'Sometimes I'm not at all sure that Nathan *knows* what he wants,' Alexa declared now, swinging her car in at the gate at the bottom of the drive that led to Farmworth House. 'He's always been driven by a strong sense of duty to the business—carrying on when my father left off. He and Dad were very alike.'

'And very close,' Rowan murmured softly. She was

well aware of how much Nathan's father had meant to him, could sense the way he still missed the older man. She had seen how his eyes shadowed, his voice deepened, becoming slightly husky, whenever Nathan Kennedy Senior's name was mentioned in conversation.

Alexa nodded agreement. 'Dad firmly believed in the tradition of the business being handed down through the generations, building a little history of its own. In a lot of ways he was the traditional Victorian papa over that—and, being the only son, Nathan had a lot more of that drummed into him than either Lesley or I ever did. I know it's very important to him, but sometimes I think it blinds him to what he really needs.'

She gave a small, wry laugh, glancing swiftly at Rowan, her eyes touched with gently ironical amusement.

'Considering that he's supposed to have such a brilliant mind, sometimes my brother can be singularly obtuse. His intellectual and business abilities may be highly developed, but in the emotional stakes he's pretty much a non-starter. Because he had to take over the firm so early he's put all his energies into making it something Dad would have been proud of, and in the process he's become such a controlled, rational creature that I don't think he'd recognise an emotion if it hit him in the face. Sometimes I think he hasn't a passionate bone in his body.'

Rowan was intensely grateful for the fact that at that moment they arrived at the house and the flurry of activity involved in getting out of the car made it unnecessary for her to frame any sort of reply. She wouldn't have been able to answer if she'd had to, her mind alive with memories of the time she had had the nightmare—the night she had told Nathan the truth.

The man who had taken her in his arms then, who had kissed her, caressed her, roused her to heights of desire she had never known existed, could never have been described as a 'controlled, rational creature'.

That night, Nathan's passion had matched her own, setting light to a potentially devastating explosion of feeling that had only just been caught in time. And it had only happened because, by her own foolish questioning, she had reminded him of what he had lost when Meryl had jilted him. His reaction then had proved that, in this case at least, Alexa didn't know her brother at all. But then, as she had already noticed, Nathan was singularly adept at concealing his deepest feelings—even from those closest to him, it seemed.

'What are your plans for the weekend, Rowan?' Alexa asked as they entered the house. 'Are you going home—to see your mother?'

'I can't afford it.' It came out on a sigh. 'I wish I could—it seems an age since I was home, but I just can't manage it. I'd love to see Mum and Bernard, I miss them both terribly, but I have to keep a close watch on what I spend. I ring Mum every day, of course, but it's not the same. Oh, I don't use the office phone,' she added hastily. 'I ring from a phone box in my lunch hour.'

'Whatever for? You can't have a proper conversation with the pips always interrupting you. Oh, Rowan, you are an idiot! Why go to all that bother when you could easily ring from here in the evenings?'

'But I'd have to keep a record of every call——'

Rowan broke off in confusion at Alexa's snort of exasperation.

'You've got to be joking! Do you think Nathan would charge you for a few phone calls, especially when your mother's so ill? Besides, your calls would hardly cause a flutter in the bills Nathan and I run up between us—after all, our mother lives in London and she threatens to go into a decline if she doesn't hear from at least one of us every day.'

'I prefer to do it my way, Alexa. Thanks all the same.'

Rowan regretted the sudden tightening of her tone, but she found it impossible to erase the sharpness from

her voice. If Alexa pressed her further she would have
to explain precisely why she was so scrupulously trying
to avoid being any further expense to Nathan, and that
was something she couldn't handle right now.

'Really, Row——'

'Rowan!'

Another voice cut in on Alexa, a deep, masculine
voice that brought Rowan's head swinging round to
where Nathan stood in the doorway. How long had he
been there? How much of the conversation had he
heard? Rowan couldn't even begin to guess, and
Nathan's tautly controlled expression gave nothing
away.

'I want to talk to you, Rowan, in my study—now.'

'Nathan!' Alexa protested. 'We've only just got in!'

'Now!' Nathan reiterated in a voice that brooked no
further argument.

'It's all right, Alexa,' Rowan put in hastily. 'I'm not
tired, honest.'

What had she done this time? she wondered, as she
turned towards Nathan, the unreadable expression in
his dark grey eyes seeming to drain all the strength
from her body, so that her steps were hesitant and
uncertain as she followed his long strides across the
hall and into his study.

CHAPTER NINE

'TAKE a look at that.'

Rowan stared blankly at the sheet of paper Nathan had tossed on to the desk, the dates and figures on it blurring into an incomprehensible jumble as she struggled to focus on it. The brief walk from the living-room to Nathan's study had seemed like an eternity to her, each second stretching her nerves tighter with apprehension at just what Nathan might want with her. In all the time she had been at Farmworth House, never once had he singled her out in this way, and after so many weeks of his carefully keeping his distance it came as a shock to her system to find herself alone with him like this in the study which had always been his personal, private retreat.

'I don't understand. . .'

She raised puzzled blue eyes to where he stood behind the desk. If only he had kept on the elegant suit he had worn for work that day, then she might have been able to distance herself from him better, been more able to resist the forceful appeal of his strong, well-knit body. But, as he always did in the evenings unless he was going out, Nathan had changed into the casual jeans and T-shirt that reminded her painfully and irresistibly of the gentle, considerate man who had cared for her when, lost and afraid, she had stumbled into his house. The pale blue of the T-shirt threw the darkness of his eyes into sharp relief, and the worn denim jeans clung around his narrow waist and hips and powerful thighs like a second skin in a way that set her pulse racing, drying her mouth so that she had to swallow hard before she could speak.

'What—what is it?' she managed in an embarrassingly hoarse croak.

'This——' one long finger tapped the paper impatiently '—is a record of the hours you've worked since you started at Kennedy Construction. Look at it!'

With an effort Rowan dragged her gaze away from the mesmeric force of his and turned her attention to the document before her. Blinking hard, she managed to see that it was in fact a list of dates and times, none of which made any sense to her.

'Are you trying to say that I haven't worked hard enough?'

She wished Nathan would explain what all this was about. She felt like some criminal in the dock, facing a prosecuting counsel who had just produced a particularly damning piece of evidence.

'No, that is *not* what I'm trying to say!' Nathan's tone was a blend of exasperation and some other emotion, one Rowan was incapable of interpreting.

'Then what——?'

'On the contrary,' Nathan brushed aside her feeble interjection,' I wonder if you realise just what hours you have worked. Look.' Picking up a pen, he used it to indicate each section of the timetable as he dealt with it. 'Nine till seven here—eight-thirty till six—nine till seven again. By my reckoning you've worked at least the equivalent of an extra three weeks in overtime while you've been here.'

Rowan's blue eyes were clouded with confusion and incomprehension as she struggled to grasp the point he was making. 'I——' she began, then stopped abruptly, not knowing how to go on.

'When you came here it was on the understanding that you would take Eve's place until she's fit to return to work.'

'And until I'd paid off what I owe you,' Rowan put in unthinkingly, though she could have bitten her tongue off when she saw the way Nathan's face darkened.

'True,' he agreed tautly. 'But that particular matter is well in hand.'

The oblique reference was the first acknowledgement he had made of the way, every month, Rowan had religiously handed over a cheque to pay off the instalments on the money she owed, the last one only the previous week.

'I pay you a fair wage, Rowan—but I believe in rewarding efficiency and reliability, and I have no fault at all to find with your work—quite the opposite. You're the best secretary I've ever had.'

It was only as her breath escaped her in a rush that Rowan realised that she had drawn it in on a wave of delight so strong that she couldn't stop her mouth from curving into a smile of pleasure. But that smile was painfully short-lived, vanishing swiftly as she heard Nathan's next remark.

'But I didn't ask you to do all this extra work. When you agreed to come here and work for me we didn't discuss overtime or the rates of pay involved.'

Suddenly Rowan thought she saw the way his thoughts were heading and tension gripped her again, worse than ever after the brief release of a few moments before.

'It isn't what you think!'

'What *do* I think?' Nathan disconcerted her by demanding, his deep grey eyes fixed on her face as if determined to draw the answer from her.

'I didn't do the overtime for extra money!' High and tight, her voice rang sharply in the quiet room, the need to have him believe her driving away caution. 'The work needed doing. I know you think I was just trying to get more money out of you, but that's just not——'

'Damn you, Rowan. You're no bloody mind-reader!'

Nathan's violent explosion, the sudden flare of emotion in his eyes, rocked Rowan back on her heels, her own blue eyes widening in shock. The raw-toned edge to his voice was so unlike his usual calm, controlled way of speaking that she could hardly believe she was listening to the same man.

'I didn't think about the money!' she rushed on vehemently. 'As I said, the work needed doing and I——' She caught herself up sharply, frighteningly aware of how perilously close she had come to revealing that she had deliberately stayed at the office in order to avoid being in the house with him. Ducking her head instinctively, she fixed her eyes on the carpet, afraid to look at him for fear of what she might see in his face. 'I—had nothing better to do.'

Nathan's low mutter was impossible to catch clearly. Rowan *thought* it was a blackly cynical repetition of her own final sentence, but she could see no reason for such a sardonic echoing of her own words and Nathan's next comment drove any further attempt to consider it from her mind.

'Nevertheless, I should pay you for the work you've done.'

Rowan's head came up sharply. 'Then put the amount you think I've earned towards what I owe you. That way, my debt will be paid off so much sooner.'

'And is that so very important to you?' There was a disturbing intensity about the question.

'Oh, yes! It'd make things easier all round. You'll get your money back quicker and——'

She froze suddenly, the strangeness of the situation coming home to her as never before. Nathan had paid off her debts and then he had insisted that she work for him in order to repay him—which meant she was paying him back with his own money. Even though, admittedly, he *had* needed a secretary to take Eve's place, it was still crazy. Just *why* had Nathan taken this particular way of resolving things?

'And?' Nathan prompted hardly.

Wanting this whole conversation over and done with, Rowan rushed on blindly. 'And then this situation will be cleared up so much sooner and I'll be able to leave here and go back home—get on with my life.'

She hadn't meant that the way it sounded. The truth was that she had distinctly ambiguous feelings about leaving Farmworth. At times she felt that she would give anything in the world to be able to go home, return to the life she had known before she had stumbled into Nathan's world; at others, that longing warred with the knowledge that she would never be able to forget Nathan Kennedy, that, even though every moment spent in his company was something to be endured, a constant reminder of the appalling things she had done, she couldn't imagine a future life without him.

Nathan's eyes narrowed suddenly, sending Rowan's heart plummeting to somewhere beneath the soles of her feet.

'Tell me,' he demanded, 'is what you told Alexa true? Can you really not afford the train fare to Carborough?'

So he had been listening before she had realised he was there. He had heard everything, so there was no point in denying it.

'I—have to be very careful what I spend. I can't go on with my life until I've made up for my mistakes in the past—and that means paying back every penny I owe you.'

'And *that's* why you haven't been home?' Nathan's voice was rough. 'Damn it all, Rowan, that wasn't part of our bargain! Whatever else you may think of me, I'm not inhuman. It's true that I wanted you to learn from your mistakes—but I didn't ask for sackcloth and ashes as well! Can't you forget that——' he caught up the word he had been about to use, obviously substituting something infinitely milder when he continued '—that man, and concentrate on the people who matter instead?'

Rowan frowned her confusion. What had Roy to do with all this? He was one part of her past she had definitely put behind her. If he ever came into her mind it was only when she remembered what a fool she had been ever to believe him.

'Do you think I don't know they're the ones who matter? Do you think I *like* being cut off from them like this? If I could afford it, I'd be with them every weekend!'

The swift narrowing of Nathan's eyes was unnerving, making her realise how much her emotional outburst had given away. For a long, taut moment he simply stared at her, then suddenly he shook his head slowly, like someone emerging from a trance. A second later, the strange mood had passed and he was once more back in control.

'Well, that can easily be arranged. Every weekend from now on you'll spend in Carborough—and to hell with the money. In fact, I intend to take you down there tomorrow myself.'

'You—— Oh, no, you mustn't do that!' Rowan protested. She found it hard enough to cope as it was, living in his house, working with him every day, even with other people's company to dilute the impact of his personality on her. How would she ever manage the journey to Carborough with just the two of them in the car?

'You can't—I don't want——There's no need for you to go to all that trouble,' she amended clumsily.

'It will be no trouble,' Nathan assured her, his smooth response strangely contradicted by the way the muscles in his jaw had tightened perceptibly at her reaction, etching white marks of some sort of strain into his skin. 'I have to see Bernard myself, anyway.' Misinterpreting the look on Rowan's face, where consternation at the thought of Nathan and her stepfather together showed only too clearly, he went on, 'I may own one of the largest construction concerns in the country, but I've still got a lot of time for the small independent.' A light of deep conviction flared suddenly in Nathan's dark eyes. 'My grandfather started out that way and I've always regretted that I never had

a chance to find out if I could do it myself. It's a
challenge I would have enjoyed.'

'But running Kennedy Construction must be a challenge, too,' Rowan broke in impetuously. 'You've
already built it into something much bigger and better
than the company your father left you, and——'

What had she said to extinguish the light in Nathan's
eyes so that they looked as dark and opaque as the sea
at night? Was it her reference to his father, or——
Oh, God! Silently Rowan cursed herself as she realised
how her thoughtless words must have reminded
Nathan of the fact that, with his relationship with
Meryl in ruins, any hopes he might have had of
fathering a family, children to inherit the family business as he had done, had been shattered as well.

'I think we've rather strayed from the point we were
discussing.'

The ironical note in Nathan's voice seared over
Rowan's hypersensitive nerves, her heart sinking at
the thought of the way she had inadvertently ripped
open the fragile scars that covered the mental wounds
Meryl's refusal to marry him had inflicted on him. No,
not Meryl, her uncompromising conscience reproved
her, making her wish she could crawl into some hole
and hide. It had been her own reactions that,
indirectly, had brought him such pain.

'As I said, there are one or two points of business I
want to discuss with your stepfather, so the logical step
is for me to take you with me when I go to see him
tomorrow. We'll leave first thing in the morning.'

He hadn't had to add that comment about Bernard,
making her feel that those 'points of business' were the
only reason he had offered to drive her to Carborough,
Rowan thought miserably as she made her way up to
her room to pack a few things in an overnight bag. She
had needed no reminder that there was nothing, not
even friendship, between them. But Nathan had clearly
felt that it was necessary to emphasise the point, as if

he suspected that she might read more into his offer of a lift than he intended.

Well, he need have no worries on that score. She had known for a long time just how Nathan felt about her, and that was something that combined with her own ambiguous feelings at the thought of a morning spent with him in the close confines of his car to make the prospect of the next day something she contemplated with a feeling that came very close to dread.

In the end, she was astonished at how easy it turned out to be. The journey down to Carborough started off badly, the effort she had to make to contribute even the most stilted comments to what might laughingly have been called conversation making the atmosphere stiff and awkward. But Nathan persisted, keeping his comments and questions light and confining them to uncontroversial subjects until in the end she found herself thawing, slowly becoming more relaxed, until she was actually enjoying herself, and once they reached her parents' home things improved even further.

Nathan fitted into the family atmosphere amazingly well. Rowan had never seen him so relaxed and totally at ease, but then she had forgotten that when he was younger he had been a part of a large, happy family group. When her mother insisted that he stay to lunch he even shared in the small household tasks, peeling potatoes, setting the table, and washing up with a practised ease that frankly astounded Rowan. He also set himself to charm her mother, spending a long time in conversation with her, his attentions bringing a sparkle to her eyes and a wash of warm colour to her pale cheeks. Both Bernard and Mrs Stewart clearly enjoyed his company so much that, on a subsequent visit three weeks later, Rowan was not in the least surprised when they pressed him to stay for the whole weekend.

By that time Rowan's weekends at home, and Nathan's insistence on driving her to Carborough, had settled into something of a routine. Rowan had been stunned when, on the second Friday, he had said that he would take her home again. She had genuinely believed that, having made his point once, he would then leave her to make her own way home from then onwards, but, whether to pay her for the overtime she had worked or because he believed that left to herself she wouldn't go home at all, he appeared to think that his acting as chauffeur was necessary, and after the second visit they settled into a routine that, if it was not exactly comfortable, was at least far less of a strain than the first journey they had made.

Only one thing might have spoiled the newly peaceful atmosphere, and that was Colin. Rowan had frankly dreaded her first encounter with her stepbrother, fearing a return to the repellent attentions she had so detested, but, amazingly, she found that he seemed to have changed dramatically in the weeks she had been away. Instead of the less than subtle digs she had anticipated, he had simply ignored her. He was rarely at home, anyway, disappearing early on Saturday and Sunday mornings and not coming home until very late. By the time of Rowan's fourth visit she had become so intrigued by the change in him that she questioned her mother about it, and the answer she had been given had frankly stunned her. She was still thinking about it when she and Nathan set off back to Farmworth, so she barely heard Nathan's quiet comment.

'Your mother seemed better than I've ever seen her.'

With an effort Rowan dragged her thoughts away from the incredible news she had heard about Colin and made herself concentrate on what Nathan had said.

'Yes, she did. I think it's because Bernard's under so much less strain—she's very sensitive to that sort of thing. But now that—thanks to you—the business is picking up again they're both a lot more relaxed. We really have such a lot to be grateful to you for.'

Nathan's offhand shrug dismissed her gratitude as unimportant, but the gesture was strangely at odds with the sudden tightening of his hands on the steering-wheel, and his voice sounded rough-edged when he spoke again. 'Gratitude isn't what I want from you, Rowan,' he muttered obscurely, throwing her into confusion.

What *did* he want from her? He'd said that he'd wanted her to learn from her mistakes, but really she hadn't needed anyone to drive that particular lesson home to her. He had wanted her to work for him and to repay what she owed, and she was doing that—but his comment implied that there was something else he wanted, though for the life of her she couldn't imagine what.

'Mum and Bernard are always pleased to see you,' she said hastily, not daring to push Nathan any further on that particular subject. 'I'm glad you were able to stay the weekend. With Mum being in a wheelchair she doesn't get out very much, so she really enjoys having company.'

A soft smile touched her mouth as she recalled how, when that Sunday morning had dawned bright and sunny, Nathan had insisted on taking them all out for the day, putting her mother's folding wheelchair in the boot of the car and driving them to one of Mrs Stewart's favourite spots for a picnic. Seeing her mother's delighted, glowing face, Rowan had thought that she would never be able to thank Nathan enough for the pleasure he had given her—but that cryptic comment a few moments earlier made her hesitant about expressing her feelings now.

'I enjoyed myself. I like your parents, Rowan.'

'And even Colin managed to be polite—when we saw him.'

Rowan's comment came jerkily, her thoughts going back to her mother's amazing revelation about her stepbrother.

'Any problems there now?' Nathan had caught the unevenness of her tone.

'No.' Rowan shook her head firmly, knowing that what she said was true. Even if Colin hadn't changed, she knew that since she had, with Nathan's encouragement, faced up to her stepbrother's threats and defused his cruel scheme by telling Bernard the truth herself it seemed as if Colin had lost the power he had once had over her. And now, of course, he had other things on his mind.

'I'm just not afraid of him any more.'

'Bullies are like that. If you stand up to them you usually find that they're weak and pathetic people inside.'

'And Colin's changed so much, I can hardly believe he's the same man. Marcia must have had an amazing effect on him.'

Nathan nodded silently. He had been in the room when Rowan's mother had explained that Colin had fallen head over heels for Marcia Alton, the secretary who had taken Rowan's place when she had left to go and work for Nathan. Marcia was a divorcee, several years older than Colin.

'I can't believe he's actually going to get married.'

'It could be just what he needs. From what your mother said, Marcia clearly dotes on him; she mothers him hopelessly. With her, he'll have his own little kingdom where he'll be right at the centre of things, sure of Marcia's constant attentions—which I gather is what he's always wanted.'

Seeing Rowan's head turn towards him, a question written on her face, Nathan continued, 'I understand that Colin's mother had a lot to do with making Colin the selfish monster he is. Bernard told me that she had three miscarriages before Colin was born, and after him she was told she could have no more children so, naturally, he was very precious to her and she spoiled him terribly as a result. He could have anything he wanted as a child, and he's grown into a man who thinks that just to want something automatically means he should get it. And he was the centre of Bernard's world, too, when his mother died.'

Nathan paused to negotiate an awkward section of roadworks, then, with the car moving smoothly forward again, he went on, 'He must have been eaten up with jealousy when you and your mother arrived to spoil his little Eden—particularly when your mother's illness meant that she got all the attention he was used to getting from his father.'

'I never thought of it that way before.'

There was a slight quaver in Rowan's voice—a quaver of shock at the thought that Bernard, who had never mentioned any of this to her, had told Nathan, a man he had known just a few short weeks, all about it.

But then there was something about Nathan that made you feel instinctively that you could confide in him. Rowan knew a rush of relief at the thought that Bernard had felt that too—after the way Roy had behaved, she had doubted her own ability to judge character with any accuracy. And her mother, too, had sensed the same thing in Nathan. Just before they had left, she had taken Rowan on one side and, clasping her hand firmly, had said, 'I'm glad you decided to take that new job, darling. If you hadn't you'd never have met Nathan, and that would have been a terrible pity. He's a good man, Rowan—a strong man, but a caring one, and there aren't enough of those around. If you play fair with him, he's the sort who'll always be around whenever you need him.'

But she hadn't played fair with Nathan; she had lied to him, deceived him terribly. Even when she had decided to tell him the truth she had only told him part of the story. Roy's behaviour had affected her more than she had realised—she thought she trusted Nathan, but she hadn't been able to trust him *enough*. And yet, in spite of everything, he was still there when she needed him. She had turned to Nathan again, wanting to tell him something of this, even though the ideas were still only vague and half formed in her mind, when he spoke again, stunning her by what he said.

'Rowan, I owe you an apology. I accused you of not caring about your family, but having seen you with your mother and Bernard I realise how wrong I was. They're very important to you, aren't they?'

'I love them,' Rowan replied simply. Nathan's apology had come so openly, it was so obviously sincerely meant, that she felt the bitterness of those earlier accusations melting away under its warmth. 'And Bernard helped me so much when I was younger— when I was lost and afraid because of my father's death and Mother's weakness. I suppose that's why I never understood Colin properly. I needed Bernard so much that I couldn't see that anyone else might have needed him too—and, looking back, I now realise that that must have aggravated his jealousy terribly. But I was pretty messed up at the time.'

'It's not easy losing a parent,' was Nathan's quiet response. 'And you were very young at the time. I was twenty-three when my father died, but it still hit me like a ton of bricks.'

In the darkness Rowan caught her breath in a sharp little gasp. Never before had Nathan volunteered anything so personal, so revealing of his innermost feeling. Automatically her eyes slid to the clock that glowed on the dashboard. They had left Carborough very late, Nathan seeming almost as reluctant to drag himself away as she had been herself, and it was now just after midnight. In her mind she could hear Nathan's voice saying, 'As soon as the clock struck midnight. . .they began to open up, reveal the truth.' The after-twelve complex he had called it—no, *Meryl* had called it that.

But she didn't want to think about Meryl now. She wanted to concentrate on Nathan, to take advantage of this tiny opening in the mental armour he wore to find out more about him.

'Do you still miss him?'

'Do you miss *your* father?' Nathan shot back.

'Yes.' It was a sigh more than a word. 'I know it happened so very long ago—and time does heal the worst of the pain—but it can't take away the emptiness of knowing that that person isn't there in your life any more.'

The dark blanket of night that surrounded them meant that she could only see Nathan nod his head, his expression obscured by the deep shadows that surrounded his face.

'There may be other people you care about—but there'll never be that one special person ever again,' he said softly. 'I think it was the loss of the future that hurt the most. I'd always believed that Dad would be around when I became a father myself—that he'd be a grandfather to my children. That sort of thing was very important to him.'

'And to you.'

It was just a whisper. Rowan hadn't wanted to think about Meryl, but it seemed that there was no way she could escape. The shadow of Nathan's former fiancée hung over everything they said like a dark cloud, and Nathan's words stabbed deep into her heart as they brought home to her just what the loss of that other sort of future he would have had with her had meant to him.

'Oh, yes, I wanted children. The idea of a family tradition was as much an inheritance from my father as my share in the business. That's why he worked so hard to build Kennedy Construction up into a thriving concern from my grandfather's small beginnings. He felt it was very important to leave something behind to show that you'd lived on this earth.'

Nathan's words echoed the memory of his sister saying almost the same thing that sounded in Rowan's mind.

'And now you're doing the same—but surely there's more to life than that?'

A gleam of moonlight caught the swift, sidelong glance that Nathan shot at Rowan's face.

'You've been talking to Alexa. My sister believes I put too much of myself into my work—and she could be right. Just lately I've come to realise that there are more important things that you can leave behind as your memorial.'

'Such as?'

But Nathan had clearly said as much as he was prepared to on that subject, and wouldn't be drawn any further.

'Do you want to stop somewhere for coffee? The motorway services are just over a mile from here.'

'Not unless you do.'

Rowan's heart sank at Nathan's obvious evasion tactics. If they stopped they would have to get out of the car and go into the bright lights and noise of the restaurant, and this new, more open mood on Nathan's part would be destroyed. She felt as if the car, with herself and Nathan in it, were suspended in a tiny bubble of time where she could say or ask almost anything, and she wanted to hang on to that as long as possible. So she felt a strong rush of relief and pleasure as Nathan shook his head and drove straight past the turning to the service station.

'I don't think I could eat or drink anything ever again. I can still feel that huge meal Mother forced on us just before we left.'

Nathan's laugh was low and soft, in perfect accord with her feelings. 'It certainly was a banquet. I admire your mother, Rowan,' he went on, his tone sobering abruptly. 'She doesn't let her illness get her down. Someone else in her position might have felt that they had the perfect excuse to leave such things as cooking to other people.'

'She always loved cooking, and she was determined she wasn't going to give it up even though she had to learn how to adapt to doing it from her wheelchair. She's a wonderful woman.' A sudden wave of guilt at the thought of the way she had risked adding to her mother's problems made Rowan sigh deeply. 'I just wish I were more like her.'

Another of those swift, sidelong glances flicked over her face. 'You know what they say—the advice usually given to a man who wants to marry,' he said, lightly enough but, hypersensitive to everything about him, Rowan caught the underlying thread of something deeper and not quite hidden. 'If you want to know what the girl will be like in twenty years' time, look at her mother.'

Was that what he had done? Rowan reflected miserably that, for her, all roads didn't lead to Rome but straight back to Meryl. It seemed Meryl's mother must have passed the twenty-year test because Nathan had wanted to marry her daughter, would have done so if—— Her mind flinching away from that painful train of thought, she rushed into unguarded speech. 'I'm not sure that's true in my case. Mum never made the sort of mess of things I did——Where are we going?'

The question was jolted from her as they came up to an exit road and, to her astonishment, instead of continuing straight along the route that led to Farmworth Nathan flicked the indicator switch and prepared to turn off the motorway.

'Just an impulse.' His tone was casual. 'I thought we'd take the quieter way home. It'll take longer, but I detest motorways. You don't mind, do you? You're not too tired?'

'No, not at all. I love travelling at night.'

She didn't care what route he took just as long as she could be with him. In the enclosed darkness of the car every nerve, every sense was highly attuned to the man at her side, the warmth and scent of his body reaching her in a heady mixture that made her skin tingle with a potent intoxication.

If there were such a thing as a fairy godmother who could grant wishes, then she would have asked for this journey to go on forever so that she and Nathan could remain in this bubble of new-found peace without the rest of the world ever intruding. Would she be a fool to allow herself to hope that Nathan too had felt something of her mood, and that his uncharacteristic 'impulse' had been sparked off by the same sort of feelings?

CHAPTER TEN

'You're too hard on yourself.'

After negotiating the change of route and circling a huge roundabout, Nathan took up the conversation at the point at which it had been broken off.

'You made a bad mistake, but you don't have the monopoly on that. When it came down to it, you faced up to what had happened and knew what you had to do to put it right. I may have given you a push here and there, but in the end you were the one who said that what you *wanted* was to go back and tell Bernard everything—and you were prepared to fight me to do it. You've learned from your mistakes, Rowan. The people who really screw up their lives are the ones who can't do that.'

Rowan suddenly found it very hard to breathe naturally. There had been no anger, no reproach in Nathan's quiet voice, only the understanding and sympathy she had seen in him from the very beginning. He no longer held what she'd done against her, so perhaps there *was* a chance that they could begin again.

'I'm never going to let anything like that happen ever again,' she declared vehemently, sensing intuitively that there was no need to say anything, but wanting Nathan to hear the words just the same. 'And if I make mistakes in the future I'm going to tackle them head on. I've learned that running away is just a coward's way out—it solves nothing.'

'It was Colin you were running away from. If he hadn't put in his sordid little blackmail attempt and panicked you completely, you'd probably have come clean with Bernard that very day.'

The conviction in Nathan's voice made Rowan's heart kick painfully in her chest. He *believed* in her;

there was no trace of the contempt and disgust that had darkened his tone so often before. But on the night she had told him her story——

In a sudden, blinding flash of revelation, Rowan saw the events of that night over again, illuminated by this new discovery, and recognised what, in her guilt and fear, she had missed before. It hadn't been her account of the way she had covered up for Roy that had unleashed the black anger in him. That had only come a short time later, when she had admitted that the story of her loss of memory had been nothing but a piece of fiction.

Rowan drew in a deep, gulping breath of air, praying that her voice wouldn't fail her now, when she needed it most. 'I'm desperately sorry for the lies I told you when I first came here. It sickens me to think of what I did.' The sudden tautness she could feel in Nathan's body almost destroyed her courage, but she forced herself to go on. 'Can you ever forgive me for that?'

The seconds that ticked away while she waited for his reply were some of the longest in her life, the tension she had sensed in him communicating itself to her so that when he lifted a hand from the wheel she jumped like a startled cat.

'It's over—all in the past.' The raised hand made a gesture of dismissal, erasing everything that had happened. 'Put it behind you.'

Then, to Rowan's complete consternation, he lowered his hand to her arm and gave it a quick, warm squeeze.

'We'll start again—as friends.'

The temptation to lift her own hand and cover his where it lay on her arm, to caress the firm strength of his fingers, let her touch wander up over the tanned skin, along his arm, was almost overwhelming and Rowan felt her heart take up a heavy, pounding rhythm that she felt sure Nathan must hear in the silence of the night.

His words, the casual gesture of affection, set up a

glow that pervaded her body, filling her with a sense of sheer delight that was out of all proportion to what had been said, and deep inside her a shivering sensation of desire quivered into life.

But then a moment later Nathan returned his hand to the wheel, and the sudden touch of the cool evening air after the warmth of his fingers brought her back to reality with a bump.

Friends. That was all he had said. Friendship was the only thing he had to offer. A few weeks, even days, ago she would have accepted that and been glad of it, but now she felt as if she had been given something incredibly beautiful, only to have it crumble into dust as soon as she touched it.

In the moment that Nathan's hand had touched hers she had slipped back in time to the day when she had first arrived at Farmworth House and the first time she had ever seen Nathan. She recalled looking into his eyes and thinking, with a mind numbed and dazed by shock and distress, that she could fall in love with a man with eyes like his. And that was precisely what she had done.

After midnight, people began to admit to the things that were really important to them, Nathan had said. In the dark hours of the night they admitted to the truth—and the truth for Rowan was that she loved Nathan Kennedy. And with that realisation came the remembrance of her nightmare and the recognition of the fact that it had upset her so badly not just because of its images of the past, but because, with its hopes of the future, its subconscious images, it had portrayed something that her instincts had absorbed unknowingly from the moment she had first set eyes on Nathan Kennedy. She hadn't known what was happening to her then, but she did now, and, knowing that she loved him, could she accept his friendship when deep down she knew she wanted so much more?

But she had to accept it. She wasn't Colin, believing that just because she wanted something it should automatically be hers. She knew that Nathan's heart had been given to Meryl and she would never have any claim on it—except as a friend, and Nathan's friendship would be well worth having.

The silence in the car was becoming oppressive; she had to say something to break it. But her thoughts were in such turmoil that she didn't dare risk any mention of her feelings, knowing that would give far too much away.

'Mum will be pleased to think we're friends,' she managed at last, though the last word threatened to stick in her throat. 'She really likes you, Nathan, she told me so—and she meant it when she asked you to come again.'

The sudden glow from a street-lamp lit Nathan's face briefly, and Rowan was stunned to see that his expression looked strangely like one of disappointment—but that must have been a mistake, because a moment later he spoke in an easy, relaxed tone.

'I'm glad about that; I'd like to be able to think that I could visit them often.' A new note slid into his voice, one that sounded rather despondent and strangely wistful. 'Your mother and Bernard are very special people, and they seem to have a truly happy marriage.'

'Yes, they do.' Painfully aware of the way they had once more, with the mention of marriage, come perilously close to the subject of Meryl, Rowan had to fight to sound natural. 'Bernard's a wonderful, caring man, and he adores Mum. I know that when my father died she thought she'd never find such a love again, but she has, and it's transformed her life. Love has a special magic that can do that.'

The last words had a distinct quaver in them, coming very close to her own heart and the discovery she had made about her feelings.

Nathan's murmured response was unintelligible, but it sounded cynical and disbelieving.

'You don't agree?'

Broad shoulders lifted in a shrug. 'What is it that song says? "Love's just a juvenile fancy"—except that when I was a juvenile I didn't go for all that romance business either.'

'But you must have believed in it once, with——' Rowan bit her words off sharply, her heart thudding violently at the realisation of what she had been about to say.

'With Meryl?' Nathan completed the sentence for her. 'Oh, yes, I wanted to marry her very much.'

The dark irony that laced his words confused and disturbed Rowan. She felt as if her heart were being torn to ribbons inside her, but there was something she had to say though every nerve cried out against it.

'Then why did you let her go? Oh, I know what happened—but why did you leave it like that? Why didn't you go after her—explain everything——?'

'It wasn't as simple as that,' Nathan cut in on her sharply. 'And since then it's become a hell of a lot more complicated.'

'But surely she must have loved you if she agreed to marry you?'

If Nathan had wanted to marry *her* and something had come between them, she would have done anything that was humanly possible to heal the rift, bring them back together. But Nathan had simply let Meryl go without trying to put things right.

'If I loved someone——' The words were choked off because she was incapable of continuing.

'But you did—you loved Roy.'

'Roy?'

For a moment the name sounded alien to Rowan, as if she had never heard it before. Her growing feelings for Nathan had driven all thoughts of Roy from her mind.

'I didn't love Roy.' Was that what he thought, that she had covered up for Roy out of love for him? 'It was his mother I really cared about.'

'His mother?'

It was too late to go back now. Nathan would never let her get away without a full explanation, and so, reluctantly and hesitantly, she recounted Roy's story of his imaginary sick mother.

'I *believed* him, and I thought I understood how he felt——' Once more she broke off abruptly as, with a sudden violent movement, Nathan swung the car to the side of the road and slammed on the brakes with a force that stunned her into silence.

'Why the hell didn't you tell me this before?' His voice was harsh and raw, searing over Rowan's sensitive nerves. 'Why did you let me think you were infatuated with the bastard?'

'I—I felt so guilty at the way I'd deceived you—and I didn't want you to think that I was trying to get your sympathy, that I couldn't face up to what I'd done. It doesn't really make any difference. What I did was still——'

'It makes all the difference in the world!' Nathan declared harshly. 'Damn you, Rowan, don't you realise how hard it's been? Don't you know how hellishly all-fired impossible I've found it having you living in my house?'

Because every second she spent there reminded him of the way he had lost Meryl and the part she had played in his personal tragedy. Rowan's hands clenched tightly in her lap and she had to bite down hard on her lower lip to keep back the cry of pain and desolation that almost escaped her.

I'm—sorry.'

It was inane, it sounded downright pathetic, but it was all she could manage.

'You're *sorry*?' Nathan spat the word out like a violent expletive. 'Is that all you can say? All these weeks I've had you near me and——'

He stopped abruptly, drawing a long, ragged breath, and when he spoke again his voice had changed dramatically, becoming suddenly softly husky, with an impossible, deep, sensual note in it.

'You're a very beautiful woman, Rowan.'

It was so unexpected that for a long moment Rowan simply froze in shock, staring straight into the dark pools of his eyes, unable to believe that she had heard him right.

'But—but I thought you didn't find me at all attractive.'

'When did I say that?'

He had never actually *said* it, but his apparent hostility and contempt for her, the distance he had always been careful to keep between them, had been evidence enough.

Through a haze of confusion Rowan heard Nathan's low, shaken laugh.

'God, lady, but you've got a short memory! That night is etched on my mind.'

'That night?' Rowan's mind reeled as if his words had been an actual blow to her head. Could he possibly mean the time she had had the nightmare—the night he had taken her in his arms, kissed her, caressed her, would have made love to her if the realisation of what he was doing hadn't struck home?

Did he really believe that she could have forgotten that? It was in her mind almost every waking minute of every day. She couldn't stop herself from recalling the feel of his kiss, the sensation of his hands on her skin, even though such thoughts only reawakened the aching need she had felt then.

The uneven beat of her heart accelerated to a wild, frantic pounding as Nathan flung aside his seat-belt and reached out to grip her arms fiercely, hard fingers digging into her skin.

'The time you had the nightmare.' Unbelievingly she heard his voice confirm her private thoughts. 'When you told me about Bernard—and Roy.' His mouth twisted savagely on the second name. 'When I held you in my arms. God, Rowan!' Nathan's voice roughened, became thick with suppressed emotion. 'I wanted you then and I want you now!'

But he had wanted her then because he had wanted *any* woman; because Meryl, the woman he had hoped to marry, had broken off their relationship and he had still been smarting from that rejection.

'But I—I'm not Meryl.'

It was too dark to see into his eyes, read his feelings in them, but she felt the way his grip tightened painfully around her arms, revealing more clearly than any words the power of the emotions that possessed him. And in spite of the pain she felt her own body respond with a speed and intensity that made her head spin, desire flooding through her veins at white heat, burning in her mind so that it almost obliterated the sound of his response.

'Meryl's out of my life, Rowan. She's gone and she's never coming back. I—— Oh, God, I have to kiss you!'

His kiss was no gentle caress, rather, it was a full-blooded assault on her mouth, crushing her lips with a bruising strength, forcing them apart to allow the intimate invasion of his tongue. But, in spite of its lack of finesse, Rowan welcomed the savage force of his reaction as an indication of a need that matched her own, too powerful to put into words. Her hand fluttered up to touch his face, waves of response coursing through her fingers at the feel of his skin, which was roughened by the stubble that was beginning to form, warm and vibrant under their tips. Then, feeling that that tentative touch was totally inadequate, she clasped his head at the base of his skull, burying her hands in the dark softness of his hair as she drew his face down to hers to deepen and prolong the kiss.

'I want you, Rowan.' Nathan's voice was a rough, thick murmur against her skin, his hands wandering over her body in urgent, demanding caresses, tugging open her blouse, closing over her breasts, driving her wild with longing. 'Come back with me now—to my house, to my bed. I want to touch every bit of you—kiss every inch of your skin.'

Rowan was almost beyond thought. She could have

no doubt that Nathan wanted her as much as he said. Every demanding kiss, every fierce caress, his quickened breathing, the furious racing of his heart, all told her that beyond question even though she could hardly believe what was happening. After those long weeks of loneliness, of believing that contempt and disgust were all he felt for her, weeks when he had never, by a word or a gesture, given any indication of the passion that was now raging in him like a forest fire burning completely out of control, she had suddenly been given the world. But how could he desire her? How could he feel anything for another woman so soon after Meryl had walked out of his life?

'Rowan?' Nathan questioned huskily. 'I need to know your answer. Will you come home with me now and let me make love to you?'

'*Make love to you.*' As the words reverberated in Rowan's thoughts she suddenly recalled Nathan's cynical dismissal of love as 'just a juvenile fancy', and it finally came home to her that, on all the occasions when Meryl's name had been mentioned, never once had he said that he *loved* the other woman.

'I wanted to marry her very much,' he had declared, not, 'I *loved* her very much.' Rowan's own thoughts about his feelings had been just that—knowing that she could never marry except for love, she had put her own emotions into Nathan's mind when in fact he was incapable of any such thing. Like his father before him, he had wanted to leave the family firm to his children, and in order to have those heirs he had to have a wife.

Alexa had been right. She had said that her brother was too controlled, too rational a person to know the burning fire of love. Emotionally, she had said, Nathan was a non-starter.

'Rowan!' Impatience and exasperation at her silence rang in Nathan's voice. 'Don't tell me you don't want me because I won't believe it. You couldn't have responded to me like that if you felt nothing.'

If only he knew that it was because she felt so much that she was hesitating. Because what Nathan meant by 'feeling' and her own definition of the word were worlds apart. Was she prepared to settle for that?

Just as, a short time before, she had had to decide whether she could accept just his friendship, now Rowan found herself facing another, almost impossible decision. It *wasn't* enough. She couldn't settle for so little! But wasn't *anything* better than nothing?

Nathan didn't love her, but then he didn't love anyone. He didn't even believe in that emotion. The desire he now felt for her wasn't even as strong as the passion he must have felt for Meryl, because he had offered the other woman marriage and with Rowan he simply wanted an affair. But then Meryl had her social status, her independent income, her position in the community to recommend her, all of which made her an eminently suitable candidate for the role of Mrs Nathan Kennedy. Without those attributes, desire was all that would hold them together, and that was unlikely to last forever. When it faded. . .

'For God's sake, Rowan! What's your answer?'

She couldn't go through with it! She needed much, much more than he was offering, and so, though it tore at her heart to deny him, she opened her mouth to form the answer he demanded.

But then Nathan's hand moved on her breast again, sending a shaft of pleasure so intense that it was almost a pain through her, her whole body shuddering in pleasure. Her mind hazed over and through the mist of delight she heard her own voice saying not the simple, 'No' she had intended, but, 'Yes, Nathan. Oh, yes!'

CHAPTER ELEVEN

'. . .AND I hope to hear from you soon on this matter. Yours et cetera.'

Nathan finished the last of the letters he had been dictating and, leaning back in his chair, stretched luxuriously, drawing his dark blue shirt tight across his broad chest.

'That's the lot, Rowan. Get them typed up, will you, and I'll sign them as soon as you're finished.'

'I'll get started right away.'

Rowan worked hard on her voice and was relieved to find that nothing of the way she was feeling showed in it. She supposed that, in time, she would grow accustomed to the way Nathan appeared to be able to keep his working life and personal relationships totally separate, but after less than a week she still found it difficult to handle. From the moment they left Farmworth House in the morning, he slipped automatically into the role of Nathan Kennedy, businessman and managing director of Kennedy Construction, and it was as if the passionate lover who came to her room at night had ceased to exist.

Still, if that was the way he wanted it, that was how it had to be, she reflected, determinedly keeping her face expressionless as she headed for the door.

'Thanks,' Nathan's voice floated after her, vague and abstracted, his attention already turning to the papers before him on his desk.

She had told herself she could handle it, Rowan reminded herself as she sat down at her own desk and automatically inserted paper and carbon into the typewriter. Swept away on the tidal wave of desire that Nathan had woken in her, she had really believed that it would be enough. Now she was no longer so sure.

But she couldn't go back. She couldn't give up what she had. Surely even the small part of Nathan that was hers was better than nothing?

The letters ignored, she let her mind slide back over the past five days, her thoughts centering firmly on the fateful night when Nathan had driven her back from Carborough. After her capitulation the journey to Farmworth had been completed at record-breaking speed as if, having won her consent, Nathan was determined to lose no time in achieving his aim of making love to her.

The house was in darkness when they arrived, Alexa obviously already in bed and fast asleep. At least, Rowan hoped she was. If Nathan's sister should hear their arrival and come downstairs she didn't know what she would say. She felt incapable of speaking to anyone, absorbed in her own feelings, the aching longing of a short time earlier now mixed with a strong dose of fear.

The near-delirium Nathan's caresses had reduced her to had faded during the drive, but the need he had created still lingered like a gnawing pain and she knew that only the experience of his full lovemaking would ever assuage it. But that didn't stop her stomach from twisting into tight knots of apprehension as, with her hand held firmly in his, Nathan led her across the hall.

At the foot of the stairs he paused, turning to face her, one hand going out to cup her cheek, his dark eyes soberly intent.

'Are you sure, Rowan?' His voice was low and huskily sombre. 'If you've any doubts at all, say so now while I can still accept it. If you don't want to go through with this——'

'If I didn't. . .' Rowan managed shakily. 'If I said I'd changed my mind—*would* you accept that?'

The swift hardening of his face sent a *frisson* of fear down her spine, but his eyes never broke the mesmeric contact with hers.

'If you say no, then it's no,' he told her seriously. '*Are* you having second thoughts?'

'I. . .'

Rowan didn't know how to answer him. If she *was* having second thoughts, they were not about whether she wanted Nathan to make love to her—that was the thing she desired most in all the world. The problem was that it wasn't *all* she wanted.

'Is it because it's your first time? Oh, Rowan!' Nathan exclaimed as she turned startled blue eyes on him. 'It's self-evident. Colin could never have got to you so badly if you'd ever made love with anyone else.'

One arm reached out and gently drew her to his side, cradling her against the warm strength of his body as he tenderly smoothed the short black hair back from her face.

'I want you, Rowan, and if you want me enough then I'd be deeply honoured to be your first lover. But you have to be *sure*. I don't want either of us to have any regrets.'

That was one thing Rowan could be totally sure of. She would never, ever regret having loved this man, even if her feelings were not returned. She wanted him in every way it was possible for a woman to want a man, and her life would be impoverished, empty, if she never experienced the sensations she now felt were possible.

'One other thing,' Nathan said quietly, his eyes still holding hers. 'I know about you, so it's only right that you should know about me. I'm no innocent, Rowan. There have been other women in my life—I'm not denying that—but I'm no philanderer, and for a long time the demands of my job took up all the energy I had——'

'I understand,' Rowan broke in, lifting a hand to his mouth to silence him.

There was no need for him to go any further. Talking to Alexa had left her in no doubt that Nathan was not promiscuous, and—mentally she winced as once more the shadow of the past crept over the present—he and Meryl had been together for over three years.

She felt Nathan's lips press warmly against her fingertips for a brief second, then he took her hand in his and held it firmly.

'What I'm trying to say is that if you've any doubts. . .'

Rowan looked straight into the depths of his eyes, seeing in them the honesty and sincerity she had always admired in him, and drew a deep, uneven breath.

'No doubts,' she said firmly. 'No doubts at all.'

Even so, it hadn't been easy. Innocent and ignorant as she was, she had found it hard to relax, the heady delight she had known earlier weakening at the knowledge that this time there was no going back. Her body thrilled to Nathan's touch, each kiss, each caress a source of intense delight, but her mind was prey to uncertainty and the fear that she might somehow disappoint him, so her hands became clumsy, her muscles tense.

But Nathan was infinitely patient, soothing her with soft words, taking the time to help her relax, easing away her fears as gently as he had eased the clothes from her body. His hands stroked her body as he had promised, finding nerve-endings and secret pleasure spots that she had never known existed until she caught her breath in sheer joy at the sensation. He held back from any more intimate caresses until he felt some of the tension leave her body and sensed that, slowly, she was beginning to respond to him. Only then did he let his hands and lips move to her breasts, their touch feather-light and strangely uncertain, as if he felt that even now she might repulse him sharply.

But by then Rowan had no thought of rejecting him. Under the sensual sureness of his touch she was melting, her restraint slipping away as her body came alive in a new, more gentle way than the burning desire she had experienced before. It was as if Nathan knew intuitively that that fierce need would frighten her, that acting on pure instinct she would fight the sensation of helplessness, of being swept away on a powerful flood-tide that threatened to overpower her completely.

By the time that Nathan's hand feathered down over the curve of her hip to rest on her thigh Rowan knew that her lack of experience no longer mattered. This act of loving was as old as time, a matter of instinct rather than rational thought, and in spite of the fact that there wasn't even the gentlest pressure from that caressing hand she let her legs part herself, sighing her need in his ear.

Beside her she felt Nathan stiffen.

'Are you ready for this, Rowan?' he whispered against her hair. 'I don't want——'

'Nathan.' Surprisingly, her own voice was firmer, more confident than his. 'Every woman knows when the time is right. For me, that time is now.'

She heard him make a rough, thick sound in his throat as she felt his weight cover her. The moment that his body fused with hers was a shock, one that made her cry out, her eyes opening wide, and immediately Nathan stilled, his hand stroking her hair, her cheeks, her throat.

'Loosen up, sweetheart,' he coaxed softly. 'I'll not do anything you don't want me to. Just say when you're ready.'

She could see the desire that burned like yellow flames in the darkness of his eyes, and was stunned that, even now, he could still think of her, put her needs above his own. The rush of pleasure that realisation brought relaxed the muscles that had tightened against his intimate invasion and her body adjusted to the feel of his until tentatively, experimentally, she moved slightly underneath him, awkwardly at first, but then more confidently as an inner, primitive rhythm took control.

'Rowan!' Her name was a shaken cry. 'Darling, don't! I can't——I won't be able to stop——'

His husky desperation sparked off a glorious, soaring

sense of delight at the thought that *she* could have brought this controlled, unemotional man to such a peak of need. With a secret inner smile she let her hands slide down the length of his back, feeling the powerful muscles bunch under the delicate pressure of her fingertips.

'But, Nathan,' she murmured huskily, her voice deliberately enticing, 'I don't want you to stop.'

'Rowan?'

For a second, lost in her memories, Rowan thought that the quiet voice had still been a part of them, and she started nervously as Nathan left the doorway where he had been standing and crossed to her desk.

'Where were you? You looked as if you were in another world. I had to speak to you three times before you heard me.'

'I'm sorry—I was day-dreaming.'

Rosy colour washed her cheeks as she saw the way his eyes darkened, and she knew that he suspected just what she had been dreaming about. But that was the sort of thing Nathan confined strictly to the bedroom— here it was business as usual.

'What was it you wanted? The Anderson file?'

He had asked her to bring it in to him in half an hour or so. He must have got through his work far more quickly than he had anticipated. Something twisted sharply inside her at the thought that while she had been lost in sensual reverie Nathan had still been functioning as efficiently as ever.

'It's right here——'

'To hell with the Anderson file!' The roughness of Nathan's voice was shocking, bringing Rowan's eyes open wide in amazement. 'I couldn't concentrate on it today. I can't concentrate on *anything*, knowing you're out here.'

Rowan barely saw his hands go out, knew only that they had fastened round her arms and lifted her bodily from her seat.

'How the hell am I supposed to work when all I want to do is kiss you?'

Before she had time to think he had suited action to the words, pulling her hard against him and covering her mouth with his. The fierce, demanding pressure of his lips drove all thought, all awareness from Rowan's mind so that it was just a glowing haze as she returned his kiss with equal fervour, blind and deaf to her surroundings. She never heard the door open, was totally unaware of any other presence in the room until a tactful cough intruded on her private world.

Dazed by the force of Nathan's passion, Rowan took several seconds to return to reality and turn to face the new arrival, and in those few moments she heard a soft, feminine voice say on a note of dry humour, 'I think I've intruded at rather an inappropriate moment. I'll come back when you're not so—busy.'

Rowan had never heard that voice in her life before, but some sixth sense alerted her, sending a *frisson* of apprehension shivering down her spine as her head turned towards the doorway. From the moment she saw the cool, understated blonde elegance of the woman before her she knew intuitively that there was only one person she could be, and Nathan's reaction confirmed the suspicion that had made her heart lurch painfully.

'Meryl!'

He released Rowan so abruptly that for a moment she almost lost her balance and had to put out a hand to the desk for support. Meryl's clear green eyes went to Rowan's shocked face for a second before swinging to Nathan, her attention concentrated solely on him.

'I—called to tell you I was back in town,' she said in a voice that hid a thousand other, far deeper things than the conventional words she spoke. 'And to see how you are.'

Rowan couldn't take her eyes from Nathan's colourless, shaken face, but she knew the moment Meryl smiled because she saw its reflection in the transformation of his features, the wide, spontaneous, delighted grin of pure happiness that spread across them as he reached out and caught the other woman's hands in both of his.

'God, it's good to see you!' he declared huskily, drawing her close to him. 'It's been so long.'

Frozen into immobility, Rowan could only stand and watch. She could see both of them now—and what she saw enclosed her heart in a cage of ice. She recognised the look on Meryl's face, the light in those huge green eyes. She knew it only too well because it was stamped on her own features whenever she looked in the bathroom mirror. Meryl loved Nathan; there could be no doubt at all about that.

And Nathan? He seemed to have forgotten her existence, his attention centred on the woman before him, his eyes intent on her face, drinking in the sight of her like a man who had been dying of thirst and had suddenly found an oasis in the desert.

'I've missed you,' he murmured softly. 'I never meant——'

He broke off as Meryl lifted a hand to silence him, and the wall of ice tightened round Rowan's heart as the two of them exchanged one of those intent, timeless glances shared only by two people who were very close.

In that second Rowan knew; knew with a desperate certainty and without any hope of escape that Nathan and Meryl were a couple. They belonged together and she was completely excluded, cut out of their private world as if she no longer existed.

'When I rang you, I never thought I'd see you so soon.'

The ice finally pierced Rowan's heart, freezing it right to its very centre so that she almost believed that it had stopped beating. Nathan had phoned Meryl. Even while he had been making love to her, Rowan, he had been trying to find his ex-fiancée, and when he

had finally contacted her he had asked her to come
back to him. He *had* to have done that. What other
possible explanation could there be for Meryl's sudden
reappearance?

She didn't feel herself move. It was as if she were
walking in a trance, every step in slow motion, until
she found herself at the door. Neither Nathan nor
Meryl saw her go, their eyes still closely locked
together.

'Well, I'm here now.'

Goodbye, Nathan. Rowan didn't know if she actually
whispered the words or only heard them inside her
head as they clashed with Meryl's quiet affirmation.
Her eyes were burningly dry as she turned a last,
lingering look on the man she loved, though she wished
with all her heart that there had been some tears to
blur and make indistinct the sight of Nathan's arms
going round Meryl's waist. Unheeded and unwanted,
Rowan slipped silently out of the door.

In the busy, bustling offices of Kennedy Construction there was only one place where she could be sure
of some degree of privacy, and, keeping her head well
down, she fled towards the Ladies', dashing into its
sanctuary like a terrified rabbit seeking the safety of its
burrow. As the door swung to behind her she leaned
limply against the wall, her body tembling uncontrollably as reaction set in with a force that left her
oblivious to anything beyond the searing anguish deep
inside her. Her hands clenched at her sides, her eyes
tightly closed, she murmured Nathan's name over and
over again in a litany of pain and despair.

How long she stayed like that she had no idea. She
only knew that, before she had regained any control
over herself, she heard a door open and close and the
tap of high heels coming down the corridor. When the
footsteps paused outside her refuge she jolted upright
swiftly, her mind going completely blank in panic
before rational thought reasserted itself and she
headed towards one of the nearby cubicles.

But she had hesitated a moment too long. Even as she reached this new hiding-place the door opened and Meryl came into the room.

'I thought I'd find you here.' The low, soft voice had no hostility or antagonism in it, but nevertheless it still had the power to sting Rowan like the flick of a whip. 'Rowan—we have to talk.'

Vainly Rowan tried to find the words to refute that calm statement, to declare that there was nothing to be said—that she couldn't doubt the evidence of her own eyes. But nothing would come and all she managed was an inarticulate jumble of sounds that brought a frown to Meryl's classically beautiful face.

'Oh, dear, you are in a state.' She sounded genuinely sympathetic, Rowan thought dazedly. 'Look, sit down.'

Moving like an automaton, Rowan allowed herself to be led to a chair, accepted the glass of water Meryl pressed on her, and even managed to take a few shaky sips of the cool liquid.

This wasn't fair, her bruised mind cried. Fate could at least have spared her this, could have allowed her to dislike Meryl on sight, to find her a hard, brittle bitch as the 'other woman' was traditionally supposed to be. Instead, as the other girl knelt beside her, completely indifferent to any damage she might do to her smart cream suit, and blue eyes met green, she knew intuitively that in any other circumstances she would find it very easy to like Meryl Freeman very much. But then, of course, Nathan would never have been fool enough to fall for the hard-bitch type.

'Are you up to talking?' Meryl asked. 'And don't tell me we have nothing to talk about, because I saw your face when I walked into Nathan's office just now. I know what you're thinking.'

'Do you?' Rowan found a voice at last, even if it was only a weak, broken croak. 'Do you know how I feel?'

'Yes, I do—because, you see, I've been there myself.'

Something in the low tones penetrated the fog that clouded Rowan's brain and she looked again at Meryl sharply, stunned to see that those huge green eyes were glittering over-brightly.

Tears? Why should Meryl of all people be close to weeping? What had happened in the few minutes since she had left her and Nathan alone together?

'Rowan, listen carefully, because this is important. Nathan and I—what we had is finished, *over*. It was wonderful while it lasted, but——'

'Oh, no! *No*!'

If there was one thing that had kept Rowan from breaking up, it was the thought that, because of Meryl's return, *Nathan* would be happy, that he and the woman he wanted to marry would be together as they should have been if she hadn't blundered into their lives, destroying their future together.

'Meryl, you can't mean that! What you saw in there—that kiss—it didn't mean anything. Nathan doesn't love me—I know it's you he wants. He never meant to jilt you—he was on his way to your wedding when I collapsed at his feet. Meryl, I know you love him—— Oh, please, you *have* to forgive him!'

'Oh, Rowan.' Once more Meryl took her hand and squeezed it gently. 'Nathan didn't jilt me.' She gave a shaky laugh. 'If anything, we jilted each other.'

Blinking hard in confusion, Rowan stared at the other woman blankly. 'I don't understand. He——'

She had been about to say, 'He loves you', but in her mind she heard Nathan's dismissal of the idea of love as just a juvenile fancy and caught herself up hastily.

'He asked you to marry him.'

Meryl shook her blonde head slowly, her expression gently resigned. 'Nathan never asked me to marry him, Rowan. I was the one who proposed to him. It is a Leap Year, remember?' She sighed, pushing one hand through her sleek golden hair. 'You're right about one thing, Rowan. I do love Nathan very much—but not as a husband, more as a very dear friend. I wish it could be otherwise, but I've had plenty of time to think about things and I know that the decision I came to on our wedding day was the right one. I see that now, but it's not been easy getting to this point. Nathan's been part of my life for years. Even before we started going out together, he was always there—our families have been friends for years. I had a hopeless crush on him when I was about sixteen, and in a lot of ways I never really got over it, so I was in seventh heaven when he started seeing me regularly. We had a wonderful time together, even if there was no great passion in our relationship, but then, just after Christmas, I could see that he was getting restless. I couldn't put my finger on what was wrong, but I thought he was going to break off our relationship.'

Meryl's smile was rueful, slightly self-derisive.

'I couldn't imagine life without him. I know now that he would never withdraw his friendship just because we were no longer lovers, but at the time I wasn't thinking too clearly—I only knew I didn't want to lose him. We had dinner together on February the twenty-ninth. I'd had a little too much wine and, without considering things properly, I proposed. To my astonishment Nathan said yes. I don't know why— you'll have to ask him that for yourself—because I knew even then that he didn't love me, not in the way that would make our marriage work. Even by the very next day I had my doubts, but suddenly Nathan was the one who wanted this marriage.'

Because he wanted children, Rowan thought, recalling the conversation in the car on the way back from Carborough. Because he wanted someone to inherit the tradition his father had bequeathed to him.

'By this time our engagement had been announced and I was on a roundabout that I couldn't get off. I buried my doubts—wouldn't even let them form in my mind. I knew that I did care for Nathan, and he for me, and I convinced myself that it was all going to work out. But then, on the morning of our wedding day, I knew I couldn't go through with it.'

Meryl drew a long breath, looking deep into Rowan's face as if willing her to believe what she was saying. But there was no need for that, Rowan knew that every word she had spoken rang with the conviction that could only come from someone who was speaking the complete truth.

'I knew the only thing I could do was to go to Nathan and tell him—but before I could leave the house Nathan himself arrived. We just took one look at each other and knew that there was no need to say anything. We both knew it wasn't right for us to get married—at least, not to each other.'

Rowan was picturing her own arrival at Farmworth House, Nathan's appearance, the unfastened tie around his neck that had led her to believe that he'd been in the process of getting ready to go out. But he hadn't been on his way *to* anywhere—he had just got back from seeing Meryl.

'I've been trying to find you—to explain——'

'I know.' Meryl's smile was full of understanding. 'My secretary told me about your calls. I took a long holiday because I needed peace and quiet to think things out. Nathan insisted that I use the tickets he'd bought for our honeymoon because he knew there'd be a lot of fuss and he wanted to spare me that.'

Her smile softened, became touched with a shadow of regret.

'That's Nathan—generous to a fault. I do love him, Rowan, and I always will—but not in the way you do.'

The water in the glass that lay ignored in Rowan's hand spilled over the side as Rowan started convulsively.

'You——'

'Yes, Rowan, I know—and Nathan feels the same way about you. Yes, he does!' She dismissed Rowan's vehement denial firmly. 'But he doesn't know it yet. That's why I'm here today. I had to get back anyway—

I've neglected my business for far too long—but I was also intrigued to find out what was happening to Nathan. He's phoned me often, ostensibly to check on how I was, but all he ever talked about was a black-haired elf of a girl who'd stumbled into his life and turned it upside-down.'

'*Me?*' Rowan croaked hoarsely.

'You,' Meryl confirmed. 'You hit him like a ton of bricks. Poor Nathan. He's not a cold man—his feelings run very deep—but because he had to take over the business so young, at a time when most men are out playing the field, enjoying themselves, he's imposed such a rigid discipline on himself that he can't even recognise love when it jumps up and hits him in the face. But *I* could, and that's why I came here today. I wanted to meet the woman who'd knocked my supremely rational, controlled friend so completely off balance that he was prepared to resort to all sorts of subterfuge just to keep her in his life. And I wanted to know if you felt the same way about him.'

'*All sorts of subterfuge.*' Rowan was trying to grasp what Meryl was telling her, her mind whirling crazily as she made the connection between the other woman's words and Nathan's insistence that she should come and work for him, his determination that she should live at Farmworth House. But he had shown no sign of any of this!

Meryl flashed a laughing smile at Rowan's bemused face.

'If it wasn't obvious that you did from the scene I stumbled on, then it certainly was from the moment I saw your face. I wanted to shake Nathan for being so blind. I wanted to tell him to get his act together— grab you and put a ring on your finger without delay.'

'And did you?' A tiny echo of Meryl's amusement had crept into Rowan's low voice.

'I didn't get the chance. The minute he realised that our old friends' reunion—and that was *all* it was,

Rowan—had upset you so much he was out of the room searching for you before I could say a thing.'

Meryl's smile widened, became a broad, empathic grin.

'I knew where you'd be, of course. The Ladies' loo is the traditional refuge of any woman who wants to cry her eyes out in private. And now the rest is up to you.'

'Me?'

Meryl nodded, her expression sobering slightly.

'You'd better go and find Nathan while his defences are down and tell him how you feel. Go on.' She pulled Rowan to her feet and pushed her towards the door. 'It's time the two of you stopped pussyfooting around each other and got down to some serious loving.'

'*Serious loving*.' The words made Rowan's legs unsteady beneath her as she headed for the door. Could Meryl be right? Was it possible that Nathan *loved* her? She didn't know if she was brave enough to ask him. If Meryl had got it all wrong. . .

But she had promised herself and Nathan that she would never run away from anything again, that she would face any problems squarely. If she chickened out now she might lose the most important thing in her life. Determination flooded through her and, turning briefly to flash a brilliant, deeply grateful smile at Meryl, she pulled the door open.

She met Nathan halfway down the corridor, just outside his office door. One glance at his face told her that Meryl's intuition had been totally correct. His expression was strained, his tie pulled loose at his throat as if he had been tugging at it unthinkingly, and his hair was roughly tousled where he had evidently been raking disturbed hands through it over and over again. The urbane, controlled, self-confident business-man had vanished, and in his place was a very human, very worried man.

'Where the hell have you been?' Strong hands closed

over Rowan's shoulders, giving her a small, jerky shake as Nathan's eyes, black with suppressed emotion, blazed down into hers. 'Why did you disappear like that? I thought you'd left me. Where are you going——?'

'Nathan!' Rowan's half-laughing protest was slightly breathless as the full force of her feelings caught in her throat. 'Calm down! I'm not going anywhere and I never want to leave you.'

But Nathan wasn't listening.

'I was sure you'd gone. No one in the building had seen you—I looked everywhere. I——' Belatedly, her words sank in. '*What* did you say?'

Rowan met that searching dark gaze with a soaring confidence, everything Nathan had said reinforcing her conviction that Meryl had guessed right. Her private delight made her own eyes glow like sapphires as she answered him unhesitatingly.

'I said I never want to leave you. I couldn't if I tried because I love you so much.'

'You——No, wait.'

Nathan kicked open the door to his office and bundled her inside, slamming the door shut and leaning back against it with the air of a man determined to repel any possible intruders—with violence, if necessary.

'Say that again,' he commanded, his voice raw with tension and disbelief.

'That I love you? I do—I fell in love with you the very first day I saw you. I love you, Nathan.' Rowan made her voice slow and clear. 'I love you.' It came more quickly this time, then quicker still. 'I love you, I love you, I love you! There.' She smiled up into Nathan's stunned face. 'Is that often enough for you?'

'Not nearly enough,' Nathan responded huskily. 'But I reckon it'll have to do for now.'

'And you?' Unable to wait, Rowan pushed him sooner that she had meant to.

The tiny pause before he answered stretched out

endlessly, straining Rowan's nerves as a tiny quiver of fear uncoiled in the pit of her stomach. Had she read his behaviour all wrong, after all? She had been so *sure*.

Nathan's eyes moved over her body slowly, lingeringly, from the top of her shining black hair, down over her slender body in the crisp white blouse and red skirt, down to her small narrow feet. Then suddenly his gaze swung upwards swiftly to lock with her uncertain blue eyes.

'Oh, yes,' he said slowly. 'Yes, I love you.'

She had thought she would never hear him say those words, had told herself that she would be all kinds of a fool even to allow herself to hope that one day he might speak them, so now she could hardly believe her own ears.

'But you said that love——'

'Was "just a juvenile fancy",' Nathan finished for her, quoting the song with wry self-deprecation. 'In that case I'm regressing to adolescence instead of finally growing up as I thought. No, Rowan——' he reached out to take her hand, his eyes very dark and deeply intent '—I was wrong—very wrong. Love is no fantasy—and certainly not a juvenile one. It's a strong and mature, and very, very real feeling, and I should know—it's got me totally in its grip.'

Nathan's free hand wandered up to touch Rowan's face very delicately, as if he couldn't quite believe that she was real, the look of bemused wonder on his face reinforcing that impression.

'You *do* love me?'

The uncertain, hesitant note shook Rowan to her very soul. Nathan, the man she had thought was so totally in control of everything he did, impervious to feeling, was now completely swamped by the force of his emotions, lost and supremely vulnerable, and *she* had the power to bring him happiness or despair with just a few, brief words.

'With all my heart,' she declared firmly, and saw his

face change as if a light had just come on behind his
eyes.

'And I love you. I love you, I love you, I love you.'
A teasing grin curled the corners of Nathan's mouth as
he echoed Rowan's own litany of love, and he lifted
his hand, counting off the phrases on his fingers. 'I
love you, I love you, I love you, I *love* you! There!' he
declared triumphantly. 'Now I've said it as many times
as you have—and once more for good measure.
Because, however many times you tell me you love
me, I'll always be one ahead of you. I can never tell
you often enough how I feel.'

'I don't mind.' Sheer joy rang in Rowan's voice.
'That's one phrase I'll never get tired of hearing.'

'That's good, because you're going to hear me say it
many, many times, every day for the rest of your life.
It may have taken me an inordinately long time to
learn how to say I love you, but——' He broke off as
he saw her smile, his eyes darkening swiftly. 'Damn it,'
he muttered. 'Come here, woman, and let me kiss
you.'

Rowan went into his arms willingly, submitting
gladly to the fierce hug that enclosed her, and lifting
her lips for a kiss that was so long and sweet and
infinitely tender that it took her breath away. When at
last Nathan lifted his head his breathing was swift and
ragged.

'I think we'd better leave that sort of thing until
later,' he said unevenly. 'Any more and I'd be strongly
tempted to throw you on the floor.' The gleam in his
eye told Rowan very clearly what would happen then.

'Well,' she made her voice deliberately provocative
'the carpet does look rather comfortable.'

'Stop it, witch!' Nathan growled with mock severity.
'Can you imagine what it would do for my reputation
if someone walked in and found us?'

'It would be something of a talking-point,' Rowan
laughed, but then the question she needed to ask drove
all amusement from her mind and, her heart-shaped

face becoming very serious, she looked deep into his eyes. 'Nathan—when did you know you loved me?'

Understanding empathically the need that lay behind the question, Nathan didn't hesitate to give her an answer.

'I knew something was happening to me from the moment I opened my door and you fell into my arms, but I had no idea what it was. I just knew I'd been knocked for six—but I thought it was the shock of your arrival and the strain of the other events of the day. I take it Meryl told you about that?'

As Rowan nodded silently he drew a deep breath and continued.

'Over the next couple of days that initial impact grew into something I didn't understand. I wanted you there with me, I needed to be able to see you, talk to you—but I didn't know why. And I cared about what had happened to you—what had distressed you so badly. I wanted to help, but at the same time I was very conscious of the fact that I knew nothing about you. Then you told me that your loss of memory was all a pretence.'

'I'll never forgive myself for that,' Rowan put in hastily, but Nathan shook his head, denying the necessity for her to apologise again.

'You were scared, lost—and after what Roy had done to you why should you trust me? I understand that now, but at the time I couldn't see it. I'd been trying to be so very careful, holding back, not showing the way I was beginning to feel because I thought you already had enough on your plate. I was quite prepared to wait until you knew more about yourself—after all, I needed time, too—but when you told me your story all that I could think was that you'd cared so much for that bastard Roy that you'd covered up for him and then lied to me, too.'

'I never loved him——'

'But, not knowing the story he'd spun you about his mother, that was the only explanation I could come up with for why you'd let him use you as you did. I was jealous as hell, even if I didn't recognise the feeling for what it was—and a few minutes later I was hurt and angry too, so I lashed out at you without thinking what I was saying. The next morning, when I'd calmed down a bit, I wanted to talk it all out with you, but you seemed so determined to get away, as if you couldn't bear to be with me any more.'

'I was so ashamed and embarrassed, and I had to put things right with Bernard.'

Nathan nodded silently. 'Which I understood—but I found that I couldn't just let you go out of my life like that, even though I felt you'd just been using me. So I made you promise to come back.'

Resorting to all sorts of subterfuge, as Meryl had said. Silently Rowan sent up a prayer of thanks for the other woman's understanding.

'I wasn't at all sure what I was going to do when—if you kept your word. I just knew I had some vague, half-formed idea of making you forget that Roy had ever existed, but to do that I knew I'd have to keep you here for some time, and I couldn't think how I was going to manage that. But that afternoon Eve phoned to tell me that her doctor had insisted that she stop work at once. It seemed like a gift from Fate—the answer to a prayer—so I rang Bernard and said I needed you to work for me, and offered to pay off the money you owed if he'd release you to come and work for me.'

Nathan was unable to suppress a wide, spontaneous grin.

'I had a hell of a job convincing him that my motives were honourable and strictly businesslike—that I wasn't a white slave trader or anything equally underhand.'

The grin vanished abruptly, leaving Nathan's face sober and obviously puzzled.

'I still don't know why he agreed.'

'I think perhaps he had some sort of sixth sense

about things. He knew that I was desperate to get back to you even though I couldn't give him—or myself—a reason why. Perhaps, in a way, I was already falling in love with you then, and Bernard saw it before I did.'

'If you were falling in love, you certainly didn't show it! It seemed that every time I tried to talk to you all I got was another outburst about the money and how grateful you were to me. I felt as if the fact that I'd paid off your debts was the only reason you stayed, and I was getting nowhere with the idea of making you see just what a louse Roy had been. Your concentration on the idea of repaying the money, the way you did all that overtime without being paid for it, all seemed as if in some perverted way you were still being faithful to him—as if you were determined to pay the penalty for his crimes as well as your own mistakes.

'I didn't want your gratitude—and I certainly didn't want you doing penance for another man's actions as if you were still carrying some sort of torch for him.'

Nathan's sudden smile was wryly appealing.

'To tell you the truth, I didn't know *what* I wanted, except that I wanted you. You'd got under my skin, and I had to have you near me, even if it was hell on earth trying to pretend that it was all just a business arrangement, which was what you seemed to want it to be.'

'I thought that was what you wanted—and that you were trying to punish me for the way I'd behaved.'

'Oh, Rowan, no. I'd understood and forgiven that a long time ago. What I couldn't stand was the thought that Roy was still there between us. There were times that I felt I wanted to reach into your heart and tear him out by force if I could. Then you told me that you'd never loved him and explained just how he'd conned you into covering up for him, and I think my mind blew a fuse with the relief that brought. I couldn't tell you what I *did* feel because I didn't know that myself. I only put the name love to it when Meryl arrived. I saw this woman that I cared about—the woman I'd thought I wanted to marry—and I knew that, important as she was to me, what I felt for her was nothing compared to the way I cared for you.'

'Nathan—about Meryl. . .'

'Why did I agree to marry her?'

Once more Nathan revealed a deep understanding of the need behind Rowan's hesitant question, a faint frown crossing his face as he considered it seriously.

'That's a tricky one. For years I'd been perfectly content. I had my work, my family, a woman I cared about even if she wasn't the great passion of my life— then, of course, I didn't believe that anyone would ever be that great passion—but suddenly I found that it no longer satisifed me. It all seemed so empty— there was something missing, but I didn't know what. Then, out of the blue, Meryl proposed. I'd just had my thirtieth birthday and, like Lady Bracknell, I'd always thought that around twenty-nine was a good age for a man to marry. I was fond of Meryl, and I respected her—she'll always be a very special friend—and I hadn't met anyone I could care any more for. And, as I've said, I'd always believed that the romantic idea of love was just a load of hype used to sell films and flowers, Valentine's cards and boxes of chocolates— and I wanted children.'

'To carry on the family tradition.' Rowan couldn't stop herself from inserting.

'Ouch!' Nathan winced visibly. 'That might have been what I said, but I was just covering my tracks— trying to appear rational and unemotional when inside I was no such thing. That might have been important to my grandfather, and even my father, but to my mind it's a bloody selfish reason to bring a child into the world.'

'You did say that there were more important things to leave behind you.'

Nathan nodded soberly, his hand curling around Rowan's to hold it more tightly. 'Yes, there are. I still wanted children, but children created because I wanted to care for them, to watch them grow and, hopefully, turn them into the sort of people who could make the world a better place. I came to realise that I wanted children who were evidence of the fact that I'd loved one very special person and shared my life with her.'

'Why didn't you tell me this then?'

'I didn't dare,' Nathan admitted honestly. 'I still thought that all you felt for me was gratitude and a strong sense of obligation—but mixed with a potent dose of desire. And I couldn't have put it into words if I'd tried, because all the time I was dodging away from the real issue, from something called love which I was trying to pretend didn't exist.'

'Alexa said you didn't know what you really wanted. I think she suspected what was happening.' Rowan's smile was gently teasing. 'She did try to warn me that, emotionally, you were—quote—a non-starter.'

'My sister has a dreadful turn of phrase,' Nathan said with a grimace of distaste. 'I suppose she gets it from those appalling American films she's so addicted to. But in this case I suppose I have to agree with her. Emotionally I *was* a non-starter until you stumbled through my door, into my arms—and into my heart. That woke me up with a bang, sort of *The Sleeping Beauty* in reverse—Sleeping Beast, anyway,' he amended with a dry chuckle. 'So tell me, princess, how do you feel about taking on this non-starter and teaching him what love's all about?'

'I can't think of anything I'd like better. I——'

The rest of what Rowan had been about to say was smothered under a fiercely joyful kiss that set her blood alight in her veins, seeming to melt her bones until she sagged limply against Nathan's hard strength.

'I think I'm going to have to give both of us the day off,' Nathan muttered thickly against her lips. 'I've found that having an emotional life can play havoc with my powers of concentration. If you knew how many hours I've spent sitting behind that desk just

thinking about you, dreaming of making love to you.
It's a wonder the firm hasn't gone bankrupt over the
last few months.'

'And I thought you were working!' Rowan cried in
mock reproach.

'You were meant to—that's why I kept the door
firmly shut. I wasn't ready to tell you how I felt—but
now I am I wish I'd found the courage to say something
weeks ago.'

Nathan's grip tightened on Rowan's hand, his eyes
black with loving desire.

'Let's go home so that I can not only tell you, but
show you just how much I love you.'

Rowan needed no second urging, but as they
reached the door a thought struck her, making her
pause.

'I don't think we'll get away all that easily. If my
suspicions are correct, Meryl will be waiting somewhere close by to find out what's happened. In her
opinion it's time we stopped pussyfooting around and
got on with some serious loving.'

'Meryl knew too?'

Rowan nodded, smiling a little at Nathan's stunned
expression.

'That's why she came here today. She said that she
planned to tell you to get your act together, to grab me
and put a ring on my finger before——'

She broke off as Nathan lifted a hand to his head in
mock despair.

'God, I feel such a fool!' he groaned. 'Everyone
around me could see what was going on and I was so
totally, stupidly blind! Well, we'd better tell Meryl that
I intend following her advice to the letter. I have every
intention of getting on with some "serious loving".'
His eyes promised that his loving was very serious
indeed. 'And I want a ring on your finger before the
day is out, because now that I've finally woken up to
the fact that I love you I want to make sure that I
never lose you.'

'You're not likely to do that,' Rowan assured him. 'I want to spend the rest of my life with you, and be a mother to those very special children you talked about.'

'Oh, Rowan—my darling!'

Nathan's arms came round Rowan's waist, drawing her close once more as he looked deep into her eyes.

'It's taken me a long time to realise what love is, sweetheart, but I promise you one thing—now that I do know, I'm never likely to forget. You see, I've learned that the only memorial that's worth leaving behind is that of a lifetime of love.'

SOLITAIRE – Lisa Gregory £3.

Emptiness and heartache lay behind the facade of Jennifer Taylor
glittering Hollywood career. Bitter betrayal had driven her to
become a successful actress, but now at the top, where else
could she go?

SWEET SUMMER HEAT – Katherine Burton £2.

Rebecca Whitney has a great future ahead of her until a sultry
encounter with a former lover leaves her devastated...

THE LIGHT FANTASTIC – Peggy Nicholson £2.

In this debut novel, Peggy Nicholson focuses on her own
profession... Award-winning author Tripp Wetherby's fear of
flying could ruin the promotional tour for his latest blockbuste
Rennie Markell is employed to cure his phobia, whatever it take

These three new titles will be out in bookshops from February 1990.

W❂RLDWIDE

2 NEW TITLES FOR JANUARY 1990

Mariah by Sandra Canfield is the first novel in a sensational quartet of sisters in search of love… Mariah's sensual and provocative behaviour contrasts enigmatically with her innocent and naive appearance… Only the maverick preacher can recognise her true character and show her the way to independence and true love.

£2.99

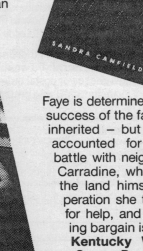

Faye is determined to make a success of the farm she has inherited – but she hadn't accounted for the bitter battle with neighbour, Seth Carradine, who was after the land himself. In desperation she turns to him for help, and an interesting bargain is struck.

Kentucky Woman by Casey Douglas, bestselling author of Season of Enchantment. **£2.99**

W🌐RLDWIDE

AND THEN HE KISSED HER...

This is the title of our new venture — an audio tape designed to help you become a successful Mills & Boon author!

In the past, those of you who asked us for advice on how to write for Mills & Boon have been supplied with brief printed guidelines. Our new tape expands on these and, by carefully chosen examples, shows you how to make your story come alive. And we think you'll enjoy listening to it.

You can still get the printed guidelines by writing to our Editorial Department. But, if you would like to have the tape, please send a cheque or postal order for £4.95 (which includes VAT and postage) to:

VAT REG. No. 232 4334 96

- -

AND THEN HE KISSED HER...

To: Mills & Boon Reader Service, FREEPOST, P.O. Box 236, Croydon, Surrey CR9 9EL.

Please send me _____ copies of the audio tape. I enclose a cheque/postal order*, crossed and made payable to Mills & Boon Reader Service, for the sum of £_____. *Please delete whichever is not applicable.

Signature _____

Name (BLOCK LETTERS) _____

Address _____

_____ Post Code _____

YOU MAY BE MAILED WITH OTHER OFFERS AS A RESULT OF THIS APPLICATION   ED1

TASTY FOOD
COMPETITION!

w would you like a years supply of Mills & Boon
ances ABSOLUTELY FREE? Well, you can win
n! All you have to do is complete the
d puzzle below and send it in to us by
ch. 31st. 1990. The first 5 correct
es picked out of the bag after that date
win **a years supply of Mills & Boon
ances** (*ten books every month - worth*
2) What could be easier?

H	O	L	L	A	N	D	A	I	S	E	R
E	Y	E	G	G	O	W	H	A	O	H	A
R	S	E	E	C	L	A	I	R	U	C	T
B	T	K	K	A	E	T	S	I	F	I	A
E	E	T	I	S	M	A	L	C	F	U	T
U	R	C	M	T	L	H	E	E	L	Q	O
G	S	I	U	T	F	O	N	O	E	D	U
N	H	L	S	T	O	N	E	F	M	I	
I	S	R	S	O	M	A	C	W	A	A	L
R	I	A	E	E	T	I	R	J	A	E	L
E	F	G	L	L	P	T	O	T	V	R	E
M	O	U	S	S	E	E	O	D	O	C	P

AM	HOLLANDAISE	OYSTERS	SPICE
D	JAM	PRAWN	STEAK
EAM	LEEK	QUICHE	TART
LAIR	LEMON	RATATOUILLE	
G	MELON	RICE	**PLEASE TURN OVER FOR DETAILS ON HOW TO ENTER**
H	MERINGUE	RISOTTO	
RLIC	MOUSSE	SALT	
RB	MUSSELS	SOUFFLE	

HOW TO ENTER

All the words listed overleaf, below the word puzzle, are hidden in the grid. You can find them by reading the letters forward, backwards, up or down, or diagonally. When you find a word, circle it or put a line through it, the remaining letters (which you can read from left to right, from the top of the puzzle through to the bottom) will ask a romantic question.

After you have filled in all the words, don't forget to fill in your name and address in the space provided and pop this page in an envelope (you don't need a stamp) and post it today. Hurry - competition ends March 31st 1990.

Mills & Boon Competition,
FREEPOST,
P.O. Box 236,
Croydon,
Surrey. CR9 9EL
Only one entry per household

Hidden Question _____

_____

Name _____

Address _____

_____

_____

_____ Postcode _____

mps
*MAILING
PREFERENCE
SERVICE*

COMP 8